Redeeming Grace

Truth and Redemption

Erin Alexia

Redeeming Grace
Copyright © 2016 by Erin Alexia.

All rights reserved. Printed in the United States of America. No part of this book may be used or reproduced in any manner whatsoever without written permission except in the case of brief quotations embodied in critical articles or reviews.

This book is a work of fiction. Names, characters, businesses, organizations, places, events and incidents either are the product of the author's imagination or are used fictitiously. Any resemblance to actual persons, living or dead, events, or locales is entirely coincidental.

ISBN: 978-0-9973426-1-1: print
ISBN: 978-0-9973426-0-4: e-book

First Edition: July 2016

Special Thanks:

To my Redeemer, my Jesus! Thank You Lord for ALL You've done for me! I will forever sing to You a song of praise. I am grateful to be a chosen servant, created to worship You forever!

To everyone: family, friends (but really you're family, too), all who have encouraged me, prayed for me, supported me... You all played a hand in this. Thank you all so much for your love!
I love y'all!! Xoxo

It is the Lord's doing, and it is marvelous in our eyes! We're only going up from here.

Get Ready!

Dear Karen,
I'm so glad for the months we spent together as housemates. I know you will excel in life in whatever you do. I hope you receive the desires of your heart as you continue in your life's journey. Never forget Jesus loves you!
♡ Erin Alexia

Prologue

Bishop Garrison sighed. He should be enjoying his vacation without any distractions. Although he stared, he barely noticed the glittering turquoise water from he and his wife's bungalow on a resort in Antigua.

"What's wrong, Edward?" Lady Garrison asked.

Edward gave his wife Katherine a slight smile. "Nothing's really wrong, I guess. I'm just thinking."

"About James?" Katherine asked.

Edward chuckled. "How did you know?"

"Whenever you're this deep in thought, it's usually about James. What is it now?"

"The silence. He tends to find himself in mischief from time to time and I fear this long period of silence is setting us up for something big."

"Maybe he's finally finding his proper footing and doing things right."

Edward eyed his wife. "While I would love to be able to give James the benefit of the doubt—" Edward paused before continuing.

"Would you?" she asked.

"...I don't think that's the case. He's been too quiet. When was the last time you talked to him?"

"Two days ago. What about you?" Katherine asked with pointed purpose.

"I spoke to him last week."

"Did you carry on an actual conversation with him, or just barely speak?"

"We didn't have time for anything in-depth. We said what needed to be said and got off the phone."

Katherine shook her head. Her husband had yet to realize that his relationship with their son could use some work. She had tried talking to him about it over time, but he never seemed to take her seriously about it. If James was indeed preparing them for something big, maybe this would be the wake-up call he needed.

Katherine thought about their children, James and Michelle. She even included Lena Wilson in her thoughts when thinking about her children. Lena and Michelle had been best friends since they were young girls and Katherine and Edward had always treated her like a daughter, especially after her parents died when she was a teenager.

A ringing phone interrupted Katherine's thoughts. After a few minutes, she heard Edward call out to her to pick up the other line.

Katherine joined her husband on the phone. "Hello?"

"Hey, Momma!" Michelle said.

"Hey, Ma," James chimed.

"Hello, you two!" Katherine smiled. "How are my babies?"

"Mom," they groaned.

"I know, I know. Where's Lena?"

"I need to call her. Hold on a sec," Michelle answered.

After a couple of minutes, Lena joined the call.

"I'm here!" Lena greeted.

"How is your trip going?" their children asked all together.

"It's going well. We should be home in a few days," Edward answered. "James, how is everything there?"

"There is some church business I need to discuss with you, but we can do that offline."

"Is that all? Or is anything else going on that we need to know about?" Edward asked.

"No sir, everything is fine."

"James."

"Dad, everything is fine."

"All right, you two," Michelle broke in. "Daddy, I know you've talked to Rand already, but things are good here too. We're just waiting for y'all to get back home."

"Lena, how is the center? How did your meeting go?" Katherine asked.

"Oh, the center is fantastic and the meeting went great! We also received a big sponsor this week, and I'm excited about how that will benefit the girls."

"That's wonderful dear," Katherine said.

"Hey Lena, I need to speak with you too," James said.

"Okay. Call me anytime," Lena responded.

"About what?" Michelle jumped in.

James sighed in exasperation. "None of your business, Michelle."

Michelle's voice turned syrupy sweet. "So James, is there anyone new in your life?"

"Don't start that either, Michelle. The answer is, no and if there was, it would be none of your business."

"Michelle," Katherine warned.

"What, Mom?" Michelle asked innocently. "I just wanted to know if James was staying out of trouble."

"You're being messy," James said. "It's not going to work because there is nothing going on. You just need to stay out of other people's business."

"I don't butt into other people's business," Michelle seriously claimed.

Everybody else on the phone paused and then burst into laughter.

Even Bishop had to chuckle. "Michelle," he said, "that is not true."

"Daddy!"

"Sweetheart, you are always in someone else's business."

"How can y'all say that?" Michelle asked.

"How can you act like it's not true?" James asked her. "The Bible says study to be quiet and to do your own business. I think you missed that scripture."

"Oh, you want to go to scripture? Well what does the Bible say about for—"

"That's enough, you two. I'm so sorry, Lena. You did not get on the phone to hear this," Katherine said.

"No apologies needed. I'm used to it."

"Sorry, Lena," James offered. "If it'll make you feel better, I can treat you to dinner."

"Hey!" Michelle objected. When they were younger, Michelle had threatened James with extreme bodily harm if he ever tried to mess with Lena, so Lena had always been off limits.

James and Lena laughed. "Thanks, but that's all right, James. We don't want Michelle to faint because you and I decided to break bread at the same table."

"Stop it, you two," Michelle said.

"You stop it," James replied. "This is ridiculous. You act like Lena and I can never talk outside of your presence. In case you missed it, she's almost as much my sister as you are."

"And that's all it needs to be," Michelle said.

"Hey y'all, I have a meeting in a bit. Lena, I'll call you later, in reference to starting up a mentoring program for our girls. I could use your insight. Dad, I'll get with you later."

"All right, son. Take care," Bishop said.

"You too. Love you. Love you, Momma. Bye, Chelle. Bye, Lena."

"Bye, James," they all said.

Edward and Katherine finished their conversation with Michelle and Lena a few minutes later.

"You were quiet for most of that call," Katherine noted, after hanging up the phone.

"I was just listening. Our son is a master of hidden agendas. Do you suppose he's trying to start something with Lena?"

"No, I don't believe so. I'm certain neither one of them want to deal with Michelle. Besides, he was open about wanting to speak with her."

"That doesn't mean he wouldn't try something in private. I'll be watching him."

"Without a doubt," Katherine acknowledged. "Come on. Let's get ready for our date."

Chapter 1

"Hey Gracie, I need you. It's really important," Dani breathlessly blurted out.

Grace was sitting in her front office in the church administration wing. Shifting her gaze from her computer screen, she regarded her friend with a smile. She knew there were varying levels of importance with her. "What level does this rank?" Grace asked.

"I'd say about a nine-point-eight."

Ah! Very important. "So, do you want to chat here or somewhere else?"

"No, I'll wait until your lunch break. I'll be with Lawrence until you're ready."

Dani breezed through the picture-adorned hallway to her husband Lawrence's office; he was the assistant pastor at the church.

Grace felt an internal sense of longing. She had long desired to be in a relationship, but she, so far, had refused to settle. It helped that she had good friends here.

Grace came to Living Word Christian Church about five years ago when she moved to Dayton, Ohio on a full scholarship to Wright State University. That had been a tremendous blessing for her because she was considered an older student at age 25. Finding the right church had been an important mission. She wanted a church with strong Apostolic doctrinal roots. She knew she'd found what she was looking for after her second visit, and officially joined a few weeks later.

Grace acquired a close circle of friends after moving from Georgia: there was Dani and Lawrence, Nathan, Lisa, and she even considered Pastor Garrison a good friend. He often told her to call him James, and she usually did outside of church. Nevertheless, she always tried to maintain a level of respect for his position around fellow parishioners.

James and she actually spent quite a bit of time around each other. Grace worked at the church, so she had a close working relationship with him, which proved to be turning out really well. Their positions dictated frequent interactions, and they had acquired an easy friendship. Aside from that, James and Lawrence were best friends, and Dani was Grace's best friend. They often found themselves in each other's company outside of church.

Grace thought about the crush she'd had on James when she first came to the church. He was a well-dressed, well-spoken, and well-educated man. All the attributes Grace found captivating and attractive in a man. His smile was marginally crooked, punctuated on both sides with deep dimples. Every time he smiled, Grace was certain firelight flickered in his eyes. He had such charming qualities about him. Grace initially found herself quite taken with this tall, chocolate man. Over the years, that crush waned into a happiness with the state of their relationship and their level of interaction. They'd gone to lunch on occasion, but that was only if they didn't have anything on the schedule. Grace did think that they both appreciated the down time and the conversation, but she didn't read any more into it. Besides, she knew her petite, thick and curvy frame wasn't his type. She didn't play herself with illusions of anything more than friendship.

Grace picked up the phone after the first distinctive ring. "Pastor Garrison, hello."

"Hey, Nylah. Can I see you for a moment? You don't have to knock; just come in."

Grace blushed, happy he wasn't near her. He usually called her Nylah, which Grace didn't know how he managed to pick up that habit, but it always made her feel special. Nylah was her first name, but everybody—or almost everybody—called her by her middle name, Grace.

"Yes, I'll be right there." Grace grabbed a pad and pen and proceeded down the hall to James' office. Going inside, she smiled at him as he stood to greet her.

"Good morning. How are you?"

"Good. Good. And you?"

"Oh, I'm great," Grace said, sitting down. You wanted to see me?"

"Yes." He handed her some mail. "I need you to respond to these for me. Also, can you draft a letter to Pastor Marks and the Praise Tabernacle Family, in recognition of their church celebration? I'll review it when you're done, and we'll decide on a gift to send to them as well."

"Okay. Do you need anything else?"

"No, that should be all." He cleared his throat. "Do you, um, have plans for lunch?"

"Well actually, I do." They were interrupted with a knock on the door.

"Come in," James said.

Lawrence and Dani entered. "Are we interrupting?" Lawrence asked.

"No, we're finished," James confirmed.

"Gracie, you ready?" Dani asked.

Grace nodded. "Let me get my things."

The guys listened with interest. "Where are y'all going?" James asked.

"Out to lunch. No, neither of you can come," Dani answered.

Lawrence feigned hurt. "My wife doesn't want me to come with her. I'll never understand," he said turning to James.

"You and James can do guy stuff," Dani teased. "And you have permission to talk about us while we're gone."

"Speak for yourself," Grace chimed in. "I'm off limits," she laughed, the others laughing with her.

As they left, James caught himself observing Grace with a new kind of interest in her. *Nah… better not even think about it.* But he was rather intrigued. He knew why, but he was inwardly puzzled because she wasn't his type. He had not really given much thought to going beyond friendship with her before.

The past six or so years had been very difficult for the 32-year-old pastor. Not long after he assumed the Pastorate position at the church seven years ago, his wife divorced him. She decided that she didn't want to be a Pastor's wife and left without notice. But not before her lies wreaked their havoc. She sent him divorce papers, and he later found out that she had remarried. It took James a while to stop his head from spinning.

Grace started working at the church two years after joining. Even though she didn't have first-hand knowledge of his situation, she was always willing to listen to him when he needed to ramble. She was naturally quiet and shy, but very easy to talk to. James had come to value the working relationship they had, and further appreciated the level of friendship they shared. They were also able to keep work separate from personal, which was very necessary for him.

That still wasn't enough though. James found himself sinking into a level of "do what I want now, repent later" type of living. He took the occasional female partner, strictly for sexual satisfaction, and yet, that wasn't enough either. He wanted the stability of a relationship, with a decent woman, but didn't think he was ready for a serious commitment because of how his marriage had ended.

James needed someone, one single person, to turn to and be that woman in his life. He couldn't get someone like that off the streets... that would be a disaster. After all, he was still the pastor, so he needed someone who could be discreet and private. He also needed to stay off of his dad's radar. Lately, he found himself considering the people he knew, and even possible friends of friends, hoping to come across a woman he could find suitable enough to be with.

The thought of Grace leaving, still fresh in his mind, other thoughts started to compound on that. *You could choose Nylah. No, I cannot choose Nylah. She might be good for me. Am I crazy? Why would I even think to do something like that?*

James shook his thoughts away and brought his attention back to Lawrence.

"Where did you go?" Lawrence asked him. "You just zoned out."

"Oh, I was distracted, thinking about something. Anyway, what's up with them?"

Lawrence shrugged. "Must be girl issues."

****

Dani and Grace settled into their normal corner booth at Smithson's Diner, with their lunch plates..

"So, what's so important?" Grace asked, sipping her ginger ale.

"Lawrence brought it up again last night."

Grace paused just before digging into her chili bread bowl. "Having children? Are y'all trying? What did you say?"

"Nothing. No, we're not trying. I just don't think I'm ready. The problem is that I'm not sure if I'll ever be. I can't tell him that, though."

"Dani, you would be an excellent mother! I don't know why you think that you wouldn't be."

"Gracie, I have no maternal instincts. But it's really important to Lawrence and frankly, I promised him before we got married that I would have children. I can't back out of that now. It's not fair to him. But every time I think about being pregnant, I have this overwhelming feeling of aversion to carrying a child. I know that sounds selfish, but that's how I feel."

"Oh, Dani," Grace sighed. "No, it's not fair to him. You need to talk to him—in depth. You have to tell him how you feel, what you fear, and trust him as your husband. And you know I don't like getting involved in your marital issues."

"I know. I just wanted to bounce my thoughts off of you. We'll figure this out."

"Of course you will. There's not a doubt in my mind. And for what it's worth, you take great care of me," Grace added, drawing a smile from Dani. "I think great friends would make great mothers and you're the best."

Dani was touched by Grace's words. She always knew the right thing to say to her at the right time. "Thanks, Gracie. That means a lot."

"From my heart to yours," Grace replied.

They finished their lunch and arrived back at the church. James and Lawrence were having a discussion in James' office when the ladies walked in and sat down.

In the midst of their casual group conversation, James, again, found himself staring at Grace. *Why am I acting like this? She's not even my type. Maybe that's what I need. No, no, no.*

Grace happened to catch him glimpsing at her and she made a puzzled face at him. "What?" she mouthed to him.

He acted as if he didn't know what she was talking about and shrugged her question off.

Deeper into the conversation, she caught him staring at her again.

She smiled with playful exasperation. "Can I help you?" she mouthed again.

James just smiled at her. He could have kicked himself for getting caught twice, but his earlier thoughts came back with a vengeance upon her return. He thought about what it would be like to kiss her... and to do other things.

After talking for a little while, Dani stood. "James, are you coming for dinner tonight?"

"Definitely." James answered, wondering if Grace would be joining them.

Lawrence followed his wife out, giving Grace an opportunity to talk to James.

"What's the matter with you?" she asked.

"What are you talking about?"

"Why do you keep staring at me?"

How do I answer this? "Oh. I can't seem to help it. That's a great outfit."

Grace was caught off guard by his compliment. Glancing down at her high-waist print skirt, paired with a red top, cropped leather jacket and gold flats, she managed to stammer out, "Thank—thank you."

James eyed Grace, intending to make her blush. He knew she was puzzled by his behavior.

"Will you be at dinner tonight?" James asked.

"Yes," she answered slowly.

"I guess I'll see you there."

Grace studied him momentarily. "You're acting strange. I don't know what's going on, but it makes me feel awkward and I don't like that."

Her straightforwardness with him was refreshing. It also helped him gauge how to deal with her on a personal level.

"My apologies," he charmed. "Would you prefer I didn't go to dinner?"

"No, that's not what I said. I just don't like feeling awkward around you."

"Well, there's no need," James said, slowly approaching

her. He stood directly in front of her, attempting to determine how the close proximity affected them. "I think we've been in each other's company enough to feel comfortable." How ironic that he was purposefully making her uncomfortable.

Grace diverted her eyes, feeling a different energy in the room. *Something's going on. I need to go back to my desk.* Feeling her face flush, she muttered, "I'll see you later," and left.

James smiled at her briskness. Noticing his own reaction, he thought some more. *She may be a good project indeed.*

Grace was excited to arrive at Dani's house and smell Dani's homemade lasagna immediately fill her nostrils. It had just come out of the oven. Grace put together the colorful salad, while Dani made the tea. They settled around the table to enjoy dinner and jest about who was going to win the game they decided to play after eating.

They gathered around the Scrabble board, deciding to play as teams instead of individually, which put Dani and Lawrence against Grace and James. Each player had their own set of letters and each word played went towards the team score. At the end of the game, they found they were tied, so they decided to play a bonus round. This time, both team members sat together and worked from the same set of letters. The first team to one hundred points would be the winner.

James sat closely to Grace, the both of them acutely aware that they had never been shoulder to shoulder before. Grace tried to silently interpret James' body language. If he seemed at all uncomfortable, Grace would probably feel doubly so. Thankfully, he was relaxed, which eased her mind.

They had a good vibe going, one that James took note of. As the round progressed, he found a way to close the distance between he and Grace, and eventually their sides were touching. The mood was still playful, so every now and then his arm would rest across her back, especially if it was their turn and they were figuring out a word. They would put their heads together and discuss their options, or she, at times, seemed to absent-mindedly rest her hand on his knee. They worked well together, smiling frequently and his touching didn't seem to make her uncomfortable.

James noticed the vibrant light in Grace's eyes when they won the game and shared a celebratory cheer and a high-five. *I wonder...*

James accompanied Grace to her car when she was ready to leave for the evening. He opened the door for her and right before she got in, he wrapped one arm around her waist and lightly kissed her temple.

Grace inhaled, surprised by the closeness she felt from James. It momentarily caught her off guard, but that was quickly replaced with a curiosity she didn't know how to handle.

"Good night," James said.

Good night," Grace nonchalantly responded, hearing the hint of a smile in her own voice.

James heard it too and smiled against her hair before releasing her. "I'll see you tomorrow."

Grace nodded and left. *What was that about?*

James watched her leave, surprising himself with his affectionate goodbye.

Later, as James pulled into his quiet neighborhood in Beavercreek, Ohio, he contemplated the perfect fit Grace would be in his life. Her subtlety and refinement matched well with the affluent atmosphere of the neighborhood. There were friendly couples and families around him, who also minded their own business. Privacy was important for what he had in mind.

I am definitely going to find a way to be with her.

Chapter 2

Grace was in the church foyer after Sunday morning service, chatting with a few people who were milling around. She happened to see her friend Nathan, headed outside and excused herself.

"Nathan!" she called out.

The sight of her instantly produced a smile. "Hey, Grace. How are you?" Nathan closed the distance between them and gave her a big hug.

"I'm good. Where have you been?" she asked, pulling away, but still in his embrace.

"Business trip. Did you miss me?" he teased.

"Maybe a little." Grace smiled.

James came out from his office. He stopped, noticing Grace with Nathan. To his surprise, the sight of them kind of jolted him. She was standing so close to him. It shouldn't have bothered James, but it had. He actually felt a little jealous. She was just friends with Nathan, the same way she was just friends with him. But she and Nathan seemed closer—like more than friends. Even if they were more, it was none of his business. *So, why can't I shake it off?*

Since dinner at Dani and Lawrence's house, James was coming to the full realization that he wanted Grace. He wanted Grace and he didn't want to share her. But she would probably never have him. The type of relationship he was seeking—thinking about—was purely wishful thinking on his part... at least concerning Grace agreeing to it. *Just let it go, Garrison.* Still, he couldn't help but subtly watch the course of Nathan's conversation with her.

"Do you have plans now?" Nathan asked.

"Not officially. You know I usually go to Dani's."

"Well, if she doesn't mind being without her friend for an afternoon, I'd like to take you out to dinner, so we can catch up."

"Okay. I'll let her know."

James felt an inner anger rising when he saw Nathan tighten his hold around Grace's waist and kiss her on the cheek. *What is wrong with me? Nylah is not my woman.* He knew he needed to cool down. Grace was headed back to the office.

"Oh! Hi, James. I'm sorry, did you need something?"

"Uh, no. Yes, but... never mind," he finished curtly. He turned abruptly to go back to his office. He got in, closed the door, took a deep breath, and he sat. He was sulking and he knew it. He needed to get himself together. He hadn't been jealous of *anyone* in years. Where did all this come from?

There was a soft knock on his door. "Come in," he said.

Grace entered, briefly observed his demeanor, and closed the door. She sat across from him with open regard.

"You're brooding," she said. "What is going on with you? You've been acting different towards me for days. Is there a situation we need to rectify?"

James leaned back in his chair. "I'm sorry, Nylah. I've just had a lot on my mind."

"You're not being completely honest with me; I'm certain of that. But whatever it is, can you just deal with it so we can get back to normal?"

What's going on between you and Nathan? Please tell me you're not in love with him. I don't want to get back to normal… I want to be with you. I want you to give me a chance. But he didn't say any of that. He just nodded.

"Thank you," she said and left.

How am I going to handle this? There has to be a way to reach her. James struggled with his thoughts. *If I decide to do this, it's all or nothing. Is either of us ready for that?* He had a feeling he would soon find out.

****

Throughout the beginning of the week, James interacted warmly with Grace, to counteract the strange way he had been previously acting. As far as he knew, she was not involved with Nathan, so he could try to pursue her if he desired. And the more he thought about it, the more he desired it. Besides, she had no idea how he was feeling, so he couldn't take his own jealousies out on her. That was not the way to win her.

Thursday of that same week, Grace came to James' office holding a stack of letters. "These need your attention. Also, both of your evening appointments cancelled, so the rest of your day is clear."

Her voice was reassuring and sweet—he loved the sound of it. He took the letters and watched her leave. By now, he had narrowed down his options of how best to approach her. Granted, he would have to work harder because what he daydreamed about would definitely be out of character for her. He knew she didn't fool around; she tried her best to live right. He also knew he shouldn't even try with her... but it might turn out to be a pleasing experience. She was private, she was a good girl, and he sensed that she might have had a small crush on him at some time. He could work that to his advantage. He would handle Nathan if necessary. James sorted through the stack of letters, but his thoughts were distracted with figuring out an approach plan. Finally, with a few letters in hand, he found her in her office. *Good—she was alone.*

"Nylah," he started. He realized a long time ago that he liked Grace's first name and started calling her by it.

She smiled brightly at him, giving him her full attention.

Yes, this was about to go down. He leaned against her doorframe and very casually clarified his schedule. "Just to be sure, you said my schedule is completely clear this evening?"

"Mmhmm. Free and clear."

"Excellent. So, you wouldn't mind me taking you to dinner tonight, would you?"

Grace's eyes grew big. "Why?"

James smiled at her inquisition. He loved a challenge. "Well, you work so hard, and I would like to show you how much I appreciate it. Off the premises, if you would allow. It's also my way of apologizing for acting strange these past several days." He had to be careful and not assume that she would just accept. He couldn't be demanding because that would drive her away. "I don't want to push, I just thought it was the least I could do. It's completely up to you."

"Oh. Well, if you're sure, then okay. We can go," she finished shyly.

James grinned, feeling a small sense of accomplishment on the inside. "Good. I'll pick you up about seven."

Grace nodded. "Okay. I'll be ready."

****

Their evening got off to a good start. James didn't have much trouble drawing her into a meaningful conversation, but he seemed to notice little things about her that he hadn't noticed before. She was passionate about her beliefs and her goals in life. She spoke with vivid animation and she had a wonderful sense of humor. *Out of all the time I've spent around her, why hadn't I seen this in her before?*

Later on, after he had returned home, he found himself pleasantly surprised at how well the evening turned out. He was also thinking about how good it felt to give her a real hug. He could still feel her pressed against him. He anticipated spending more time with her. He was also anxious to determine his next move.

James and Grace got together outside of church more frequently. Each time they seemed to grow a little closer. If they went out somewhere, it would be to little-known spots. He would end every outing by escorting her upstairs to her apartment door. They always hugged and he gave her little kisses, either on her hand, forehead, or on her cheek.

James made sure they talked every night. He also implemented spending the evening in. Either she would cook for him or he would cook for her. That soon became the majority of their time spent together, alone at each other's home. That time alone became a special secret only they shared.

****

Katherine was home thinking about her son. James had been on her mind heavily. *Edward might be right; something must be going on with him.* She decided to call and see how he was doing.

"Hey, Mom," James smiled. He leaned back in his chair, glad to hear from her. His mother was one of his most favorite people in the world.

"James! How are you, son? Are you doing all right?" she asked.

"Yes ma'am, I'm doing well. To what do I owe the pleasure of this call?"

"I've been thinking about you, so I decided to see how you were."

"All is well. I've just been trying to work hard and handle my business. As dad can attest, it's a tough job but worth the work."

James was actually a gifted pastor, which had caught them all by surprise. The church received him warmly, as he was a people person. Prior to that, and after getting his Master's degree in Mathematics, he spent time as an educator. Early on, after accepting the offer to become pastor, he maintained both his job and the pastorate, which he was grateful for. The business of both jobs helped get him through his divorce. The church rallied around him when his ex-wife left, bringing them closer together as a family. Now he was pastoring full-time, and the church flourished under his natural leadership abilities.

"Well, that sounds wonderful, dear," Katherine said. "Do you plan to visit anytime soon? We'd love to see you." Katherine missed him living close to home. Though Ohio wasn't far from Indianapolis, it was still far enough to have to plan for a visit.

"I'd love to see you too. Hopefully, I'll be able to figure out a time in the near future." What James couldn't verbalize was his desire to not interact with his father at this time. He was just settling into his plan with Grace.

"All right. Well, I know you have work to do... We love you."

"I love you too, Mom. Give my love to everybody. Take care."

"You too. Bye, son." Hanging up, Katherine contemplated their brief conversation. Edward was right; something was going on with him. He was way too easy-going. Not to say that he was normally high-strung, but he sounded very smooth, like "cover-up" smooth. *If only I knew what it was...* She decided to go pray, knowing God would know just what to do.

Chapter 3

About three weeks after they started dating, James and Grace were out, away from the city. They had already finished dinner and were chatting with another couple before leaving.

"It was a pleasure to meet you and your wife," the gentleman said to James. "We hope you enjoy the rest of your evening."

Grace smiled as she started to correct him. "Oh, well we're—"

"Delighted to meet you as well," James finished, glancing at Grace, knowing what she was trying to do. He reached to shake the gentleman's hand. "You have a good night."

As soon as they were gone, Grace turned to James with bewilderment written across her face.

"How come you didn't let me correct him?"

"I just decided to let him think what he already assumed."

"Why?" Grace asked curiously.

"Because I wanted to," James answered with a mischievous smile. "You ready?"

Grace nodded as James offered his arm, through which she linked hers. It was a beautiful night, so they went for a short stroll. They were silent at first, but surrounded by a swirl of emotions.

"I have tremendously enjoyed spending time with you, James." Grace smiled.

"Really? Wait. Do I detect a 'but'? Are you letting me down easy?" James teased, privately hoping it wasn't true.

"No, not at all. I'm just… surprised. Pleasantly so."

"Did you not think I could be interested in you?" James asked.

"Maybe I figured that you *wouldn't* be interested in me."

James took in her demeanor: her body language was relaxed, her facial expression was genuine—the smile that was both on her lips and in her eyes. He had wanted to kiss those lips for weeks now. Run his fingers through her hair. He may get his chance tonight.

"And here I was, hoping I wasn't second best in your life," he hinted.

Grace tilted her head thoughtfully. "Second to whom?"

"Nathan. The two of you are pretty close."

Grace regarded him curiously. "Nathan and I are just friends."

"Maybe on your end, but I'm not so sure about him. I see how he is around you, the way he touches you." James tried to make sure he didn't sound too irritated, but thinking about Nathan with Grace was unpleasant.

Grace raised her brow slightly, taking in his observation. "You've noticed?"

"Well, I did a few Sundays ago."

Grace recalled that Sunday and how James was acting. "OH! You were *jealous*?" she asked with dawning. "No wonder," she murmured. "Although, I do find that interesting."

"How so?" James asked.

"Why do you feel the need to be jealous? In case you hadn't noticed, I don't spend any of my free time with Nathan..." she trailed off.

James smiled at her, understanding her statement. They made their way back to the car. "For the record, I don't spend any of my free time with anybody else either," he affirmed.

Grace beamed at him. He loved her smile. Her freckle-splashed cheekbones lifted towards her deep brown eyes. It was bright, full, and welcoming... it put him at ease. They made small talk on the way back to her apartment, but James was simultaneously considering his next move.

At her apartment, James said, "Well wife, I guess this is where we part ways... at least until the next time."

Grace chuckled as she shook her head. "You are so bad," she playfully teased as she sub-consciously placed her hand on his chest.

You have no idea, he thought, feeling his flesh getting worked up as he pulled her into a hug. He pulled away slightly and pushed her hair back as he held the side of her face. He leaned in slowly, careful to gauge her body language as he lowered his face to hers. She slightly leaned into him, granting him the access he desired. He kissed her thoroughly on the lips, holding it for an added intimate effect.

He pulled apart from her just to get a sense of what she wanted. As he ran the backs of his fingers up the side of her jaw to her ear, and then slowly ran his fingers through her hair, he searched her smiling eyes. Perfect. Access granted.

James kissed her again, first softly, but then he expertly transitioned into a passionate kiss. He felt her arm curve around his neck as her other hand moved up to hold the back of his head. He slid his arm around her waist, sealing their bodies together for the duration of the kiss.

James had no desire to stop, but he felt their bodies sway

and he felt the urge to go exploring. He needed to stop now because he didn't want to ruin things. It was too soon to go further; they needed about three more outings and a little bit more physical contact. They ended the kiss, but did not separate from each other. Grace sighed heavily and James, still holding her, whispered goodnight in her ear. He didn't want to leave. He wished she would invite him in to stay, but he knew that wasn't going to happen.

Grace released herself from him and opened her door. She turned back to James and leaned in for one final kiss, short, simple and meaningful. She lightly caressed the side of his face, her thoughts racing. "Goodnight," she said before going inside.

****

James had just sat in his car when his phone vibrated.

"Hello," he answered.

"You sound cheery. What are you doing?"

"Hey, Chelle. I'm on my way home. What's going on?"

"What are you up to?" she asked.

"What do you want?" he returned.

"Aren't you glad to hear from your little sister?" Michelle asked.

"Always," James answered sardonically. "Because you just love to call me for no reason at all."

"I just wanted to say, hi. We haven't talked in weeks. Is everything okay?"

First his mom called, and now his sister. What was this about? Did they know he was up to something?

"Sure, everything is fine. What about the family? How are Rand and my two nieces?"

"They're all okay. Rand asked about you too. Are you visiting soon?"

"Well, there is always the option of you visiting me," James added.

"We can't get away right now. I'm helping Lena with a project for the girls. What, you didn't know that?" she asked sarcastically.

"How would I? You act like Lena and I talk all the time now. And you can never get away. I told Mom I would let her know if I plan to visit." James paused to start his car, wondering how to get Michelle off the phone. "By the way, how is Lena?"

Michelle gritted her teeth. "She's doing well. I'll tell her you asked."

"I could just call and ask her myself." James was needling Michelle on purpose. *If she's going to call me on a mission, I'll make her pay for it this time.*

"All right, well, I won't keep you; I'm done talking to you for tonight. Stay out of trouble James. Do you hear me?"

"Yes, ma'am. You know me." *No, she doesn't know. If she knew, she would have said something to me about it.*

Michelle sighed. "That's what I'm afraid of."

Chapter 4

Grace curled up on her couch, waiting. James had called her a little while ago, asking to come over. She aimlessly glanced around her apartment, somewhat deep in thought. Her apartment was a cozy one bedroom, with just enough space for her to live comfortably. She chose her décor using her favorite nude eye shadow palette as inspiration, adding pops of color where needed. It was a beloved combination of classic, modern, and vintage that highlighted her personality.

Grace had not expected the presence of another person in her personal space. To her surprise, James' presence there never bothered her. She kind of liked having him around. Smiling at the thought, she heard her doorbell ring. She opened the door, and there stood James in the hallway, holding a bag of takeout.

"Hungry?" he asked.

She smiled and nodded, moving to the side so he could come in. He kissed her affectionately on the cheek before following her into the kitchen, making small talk along the way.

"Thanks for letting me stop by," he said as Grace onced him over from behind. He appeared relaxed in jeans and a button down. "I was hoping you wouldn't have any plans for today."

Grace observed him with intrigue. Two months ago she had been mostly accustomed to dealing with him only in a professional setting. They talked often, mostly because of their respective positions, along with the fact that they had the same circle of friends.

Although they did share a friendship, she wasn't used to him being this… ahem… *friendly* with her. They had gone out several times and shared a few light pecks, but nothing could have prepared her for what happened last night.

It was late Saturday evening when they had gone out to dinner and took a stroll before he brought her home. When they got back to her place, he kissed her goodnight… but this one was full of passion and desire. One like she had never experienced before. She returned it with the same intensity, neither of them willing to break first. Finally, they pulled apart and he left smiling.

Grace had been wondering for the past several weeks, if she was dreaming. James was handsome and charming and she had the occasional thought of them going out to dinner on a casual level, but she could have never anticipated having this type of relationship with him.

Seeing James now, sitting on her couch, Grace didn't know what had happened. She had gone from the administrative assistant and friend of Pastor Garrison, to what felt like the girlfriend of James, in a matter of weeks. She had to admit; it kind of made her giddy on the inside. She didn't know how long it would last, but as long as he was willing to spend time with her, she would take it. She knew she wasn't his type, but he didn't seem to mind, so why should she?

"Nylah," James called to her, snapping her out of her daze. "Are you going to make me sit over here by myself?"

Grace smiled at him, giddy all over again. "No, I'm coming." Her blue sleeveless maxi dress flowed with her when she walked. Her mocha cardigan added an always-desired neutral touch to her outfit. Her straightened hair was down and free.

"Please, hurry up," James said.

Grace sat, careful to leave distance between them.

James took note of the distance and decided to slowly work his way into closing it. "How has your day been?"

"Good and quiet. I've had a chance to do a lot of thinking."

"About what, if you don't mind my asking?"

Grace paused before answering him. "What are we doing?"

"Right now? Talking," James playfully answered.

She gave him a little nudge and laughed. "Come on, James. You know what I mean."

James let out a sigh. "I like spending time with you. I like talking to you. And after last night, I've found that I really like kissing you," he finished directly.

Grace blushed deeply. She didn't even know how to respond to his statement.

James closed the space between them and slid his arm around her waist. This was a crucial moment. Either she would get up and move away from him, indicating that they needed more time, or she would stay there, signaling that she didn't mind being close. That would prove them to be right on his schedule. She repositioned her body to face him and placed her arm around his shoulders.

"What's going to happen with us?" Grace asked him.

"I don't know. How about we don't try to figure out the future right now, we just go with the flow. Is that all right?"

Grace nodded. "Yeah. We can do that." She grazed his face with her hand and leaned in to give him a quick kiss.

James was not about to let her go that easily. He took over and soon they were leaning back on her couch, enthralled in a full make out session.

Grace felt like she was melting beneath him. She became so lost in what they were doing; she hadn't noticed James' hand lightly exploring her body. When she finally did, she felt an inner struggle between stopping and continuing what they were doing. It felt good to be wanted, but at what cost? They shouldn't be this close; Grace knew it was wrong and she slowly came to the conclusion that she should stop him. Otherwise...

Grace tried to get her body to cooperate with her thoughts. The more he kissed her, the more she wanted. She instinctively pulled him closer, offering him more control and he seized the opportunity with a deep kiss that seared her senses. *How good it would feel to indulge this pleasure.* Right after that thought she heard a loud ringing in her ear.

"James... wait... James," Grace breathed in between kisses. She didn't want him to stop, but she had to try. "James, we have to stop."

He slowed down, but didn't come to a complete halt.

Uggghhh! If there was ever a time when her spirit was willing, but her flesh was weak, this was it. The ringing in her ear got louder and she felt a surge of strength to push James off of her.

"NO!!! We can't do this!" Grace sat up and tried to catch her breath. Her mind and heart were racing and she was on the verge of tears, feeling every emotion possible. She stood, fixed her clothes, and tried to think of the right words to say. She was inwardly mortified at their actions. *Oh, my goodness!!! I can't believe myself right now...* She turned to face James who had finally sat up, and was staring at the floor. *He has got to get out of here!*

"You have to leave. You have to leave now," she told

him.

James seemed contrite when he stood and slowly came toward her. "I'm sorry, Nylah. I got—carried away. I don't... I don't know what happened. I'm sorry."

He tried to reach out to her, but Grace moved away from him, making sure he wasn't able to touch her. Her tears spilled over as she reinforced her position. "No. Don't. Do not touch me anymore, please. Just... I need you to go, James. Go," she was pleading with him, praying that he would listen to her.

"Nylah—"

"GET OUT!" she yelled back at him. They both flinched at her outburst. Grace turned away from him, ashamed. She was having a hard time with the conflicting feelings and desires swirling around on the inside of her. Yelling at him seemed to be a defense mechanism, pushing him away. That would keep her from doing what her body wanted, which was to let him hold her... amongst other things.

James headed to the door. "I really am sorry," he said before leaving.

Grace sat in the corner of the sofa, curled into a ball and cried. *How could I let something like this happen? This is not good. And now... how do I stop wanting more?*

****

James arrived home, upset with the recent turn of events. He really was sorry about what had happened with Grace. It was too soon, and she didn't know how to take it. He had only meant to kiss her. She was incredibly passionate and he couldn't wait to see how that unfolded intimately. He had a feeling her quiet nature wouldn't hold for long in the confines of a bedroom and that thought nearly drove him wild. The problem now was that she may not come near him again.

Leave her alone.

James was... startled at first. He heard the voice, in unmistakable clarity, but he did not respond.

Do not compromise her integrity.

"I feel that it may be too late for that," James admitted.

If you want to be with her, then you need to marry her first.

Whoa. James was thoughtful for a moment. "I'm not ready for that again."

Then you're not ready to be with her. James, you are a pastor. You are willingly creating a mess nobody wants to be in. If you want to damage yourself, that's your choice. But do it without Grace.

"I need her. She can keep me grounded."

I said no. Leave her alone, God warned.

"I know this is wrong, but—"

There are NO buts! If you insist on being disobedient, then you must insist on living with the consequences. And there will be consequences.

James agonized over the exchange. The realness of his choice was right in front of his face. He knew what he should choose. He also knew what he probably would choose.

****

The next morning, Grace found herself conflicted and emotional about James. At church, she managed to avoid any physical or verbal contact with him, but not eye contact. That was almost enough to send her into another breakdown. She had to hold it together.

After service Dani pulled her aside. "Girl, what's wrong with you?"

Grace felt her heart beating fast as she tried to keep her cool. "What do you mean?"

"You're acting all nervous. What gives?"

"Oh... that. Yeah, I just had a different kind of day yesterday. You know, women issues. Nothing to worry about," Grace finished, hoping her friend would accept her explanation.

"Oh. Okay... Well, dinner is in an hour and James is coming over."

Grace felt the blood rush to her ears... and to other places. "Umm, I think I'm just going to pick something up and go home."

"Aww Gracie, why? You always come over. Are you sure you're okay?" Dani sounded a little cheerless. She always enjoyed the girl time they shared.

Grace felt guilty, for more than one reason. Sunday afternoons were often one of their times to hang out but she couldn't tell Dani about James. "I'm just a little tired, that's all."

"Well, come over and eat, at least. We don't even have to sit with the guys; we can go outside and keep to ourselves if you don't want to talk. Please, Gracie? For me?" she begged, batting her lashes.

I can't tell her no, Grace thought. *Besides, this is my mess. I have to find a way to deal with it appropriately.* "Okay, okay," Grace conceded, smiling at her friend. "I'll come. But I would like to keep away from the guys today. Just you and me, outside."

"Yes! Come on!" Dani said, pulling Grace with her.

At the house, James kept stealing glances at Grace. She again managed to avoid his company by staying outside with Dani. He wanted to talk to her, but he realized it was neither the time nor place. He did try though, when they had both been in the kitchen.

"Nylah," James whispered.

Grace ignored him the first time and reached for a plate.

"Nylah," James whispered again, reaching for the same plate.

Their hands touched, both of them feeling a spark pass between them. Grace's eyes grew wide and she darted a glance up at him.

"You hear me calling you. Why are you avoiding me?"

Grace made sure neither Dani nor Lawrence were

near them. "I don't want to talk about this right now," she said in a low voice.

"You can't avoid me forever," James said.

"Get away from me, James," she said through a gritted smile.

"Just—"

"Ugggghhh..." Grace sighed before exiting the kitchen to find Dani.

James stared at her in disbelief as she left.

"Man, you seem distracted. What's going on?" Lawrence asked entering the kitchen moments after Grace left.

James sighed heavily. "Just got a lot on my mind. You know how I get with that."

Lawrence smiled at his friend. If he didn't know any better, he'd think that his friend's distraction had something to do with a lady. Finding out who, would be the trick. James was seriously guarded when it came to matters of the heart. He decided the forward approach would be best. James never cared to beat around the bush.

"Who is she, man?"

James started to say something and then stopped himself. Glancing behind Lawrence outside, he said, "I can't tell you. Besides, she's out of my league. It's best for me to just forget about it. You know; leave it alone."

Lawrence raised his brows. "Someone we know?"

James managed to maintain a casual manner. "I'd rather not say..."

"All right. All right, I'll drop it... for now," Lawrence said.

Chapter 5

Later that week, James sat in his office. He was thinking about his dad... and thinking about Grace. He had spoken to his father about church business last week. Towards the end of their conversation, his dad asked him outright if he was trying to start something with Lena.

James acted surprised by the question, and he was glad to be able to answer it honestly. In truth, he knew that asking to speak with Lena privately would raise his dad's antenna. That would keep him preoccupied enough for James to implement his plan with Grace without his dad being all over him. That was working out better than he had hoped.

Grace, on the other hand... that was not going well. Throughout the week she had only interacted with him for business purposes. They needed to talk, but he didn't want to push her. From the time they started seeing each other more informally, he had gotten used to talking to her every day.

Seeing her always made him want to touch her, hug her... and more. He had grown quite fond of her. Now there was a distance between them, one that he didn't like. At all. His thoughts were interrupted by a knock on the door.

"Come in." He watched Grace enter, cautious and... emotional, maybe. "Hey," James greeted with concern. "Are you okay?" He stood and came around his desk to face her.

Grace swallowed the threat of tears. "It's just—I, umm—" She sighed. Her eyes glossed as she wrapped her arms around his neck. Mildly elated when he pulled her close and held her tightly, they both exhaled.

"I've missed you," he murmured. Even though his objective had been for them to become lovers, he found himself musing over how true his words and feelings for her were.

"I've missed you, too," she said quietly. They held each other for a few minutes more, not wanting to let go, but eventually having to.

They pulled away and James framed Grace's face with his hands. "Listen, I—"

"No, James. Not now, please." Her eyes gently pleaded with him.

"Okay." He gazed intently at her, wondering what would come next. He dropped his hands and stepped away from her, feeling the need for physical distance. She must have felt it too because her faced became flushed.

"Uhh, you can come for dinner later... if you'd like," she spoke with a quiet shyness, reminding him of when he first asked her out to dinner.

"Yeah. I would love to."

After a few quiet moments, he reached his hand out to her. She hesitated briefly before taking it. He stepped closer to her, wrapped his other arm around her waist and kissed her temple.

"Thank you," he told her. At that moment, he felt as if he would do anything for her. He realized that he cared deeply for her and didn't want to hurt her.

"You're welcome," she said. *I am falling in love with this man. But can I trust him not to hurt me?* She gently squeezed his hand before releasing it and he released his hold on her.

"I'll see you later," she said, turning to leave.

He nodded and grinned. "Later."

She maintained her reserved demeanor but he saw the smile in her eyes. Maybe he hadn't lost her after all.

After dinner Grace and James lay reclined on the sofa. James was massaging Grace's scalp, trying to get her to relax. She was stretched out next to him and he felt the tension in her body. He had to be careful how he touched her. Since she made no effort to move, he just followed her lead.

"Are you ready to talk about it?" he asked her.

"I don't really want to, but perhaps we should," she answered, lifting up to search his face.

"It's completely up to you," he said, staring into her eyes.

She held his gaze for a moment wondering. "I don't know where to start."

"Well, how do you feel?"

"Conflicted. And I don't know what to do."

I know what I would like to do, James thought, clearing his throat. "About what?"

Grace sat up off of James, pulling him up with her. "What is going on with us? How did this happen? We had a very pleasant, casual friendship, and a solid working relationship. Now we're a lot closer than I thought we would ever be, we're affectionate, secretive and unfortunately, we have put ourselves in a very precarious position. We're too close, physically speaking, but even more than that—"

James kissed her with smoldering perfection. It took Grace a moment to realize she wasn't talking anymore. Then she felt her body relenting to James, succumbing under the swift heat she felt rising within her. *Not again*, she inwardly sighed.

Grace just did not understand how he was able to have such an effect on her, causing her body to act against her will. By the time he ended their kiss, she was practically sitting on James' lap, their upper bodies intimately intertwined. Grace rested her head against his and tried to remember what she had been talking about.

"You are incredible," James said.

He was stroking her spine and Grace once again found herself on the verge of tears. It was all too much. She stood and moved across the room.

"What's wrong, Nylah?"

Grace turned to James, her tears spilling over. "This is not good. We can't keep doing this, James."

"I don't know what to say. I'm sorry for making you uncomfortable, but… I'm not sorry for wanting to be close to you." James came to Grace and took her hands. "You've become essential to me in many ways, and I have no intention of letting you go without a fight. That's what you mean to me," James finished, kissing her forehead.

Grace separated from him. "You would make this harder for me than it has to be. James, we are not being careful, and that does not speak well of us. We both know better. How can we expect to be any kind of good example for the youth if we're doing what we tell them not to do?"

"Is it that hard for you to admit that you like me?" James smiled.

"I think we are well beyond that admission. That's not the point."

James started towards her. "So, what is your point?" he asked as he reached her. He encircled her waist with his arm, waiting for her answer.

"You're not listening to me. This is serious, James," Grace groaned, pushing away.

"What do you want me to say?" James asked.

Grace stared at him incredulously. "I want you to say that I'm right. That you know it's wrong. That we have to stop before we get into trouble."

"You're right," James said. "This is wrong and we have to stop before we get into trouble."

Grace sucked her teeth, exasperated. "Stop it. Don't do that, James. Don't play with me."

"What? You told me what you wanted me to say and I said it. It doesn't appear to have helped though."

Grace turned away from him in frustration. She didn't like the effect his presence—his touch had on her. She didn't like the increasing sense of comfortableness they fell into around each other. And she didn't like what she felt and knew was wrong: she wanted to be with him.

James eased up behind her and wrapped his arms around her. "I'm sorry," he whispered in her ear.

Grace didn't have the energy to push him away this time. She didn't even want to. She closed her eyes, leaned back into him and let him hold her. His arms were strong and she felt good in his embrace. She felt a sense of relaxation sweep over her as he continued to whisper in her ear.

"I'll take care of you," he whispered.

"You promise?" she asked, turning to face him.

He tightened his hold on her, drawing her close to him. "I promise," he said.

Grace wasn't sure how long he kissed her, but when he pulled away, saying he should go, she recognized that she didn't want him to. That alarmed her, which enabled her to let him go. This time…

****

"Hey, girl!"

Grace smiled into her phone, mentally checking her tone. "Hey, Dani! What's up, girl?"

"Not much. Where are you?"

"I'm out—running some errands."

"Oh. How come you didn't call me?"

Because I'm out of town with James. And I'm shopping for our date on Friday evening. "Oh, I didn't want to bother you. I was already out, so I just decided to take care of some things. And you know sometimes I just need 'me' time."

James came up behind her and kissed behind her open ear. "So, now I'm 'me time?'" he whispered. Grace turned to face him, making a face and putting her finger to his mouth.

"Well, I feel like we haven't spent much time together lately," Dani said. "I miss my friend."

"Oh honey, I miss you too! We'll get together soon. I've just been preoccupied lately," Grace finished, shooting James a warning glance as he held her suggestively. They had become even more physically comfortable around each other. Last night had been... well... Grace blushed at the memory.

"I just have this feeling, Grace. Are you sure you're okay?"

Uh-oh. "Yes honey, I'm fine," she said pushing away from James. "You don't need to worry."

"If you say so." Dani gave a weighted pause, and then, "Well, call me later, okay?"

"All right. Love you, girl!"

"Love you, too. Bye."

Grace hung up and turned to James. "She has a feeling."

"About us?" James asked, his brows raised.

"No, I don't think so. More about me. You know how she gets with her "feelings." She'll pry until she finds out what she wants to know."

"Are you going to tell her?"

"No. I don't want her to know." That revelation kind of shook Grace. She usually was able to confide anything to Dani. "Have you mentioned anything to Lawrence?"

"Not really." James rushed to continue when he saw Grace's face. "A few Sundays ago, at their house, he picked up on my mood. That was the day after our encounter."

"Yes, I remember. What happened?"

"He just asked me who was the lady on my mind. I told him it was someone who was out of my league. He asked another question and I just relayed that I couldn't tell him who it was. For obvious reasons, I didn't want to get into a discussion about you, or us. He dropped it after that, but I know he still wonders."

"Are we going to keep this between us? I don't want people in our business," Grace declared.

To which is one of the reasons why I picked you. "This will definitely stay between us. It will be our secret." James gave her a lingering kiss on the lips, glad to be able to show some public affection. James planned to lay it all on the line Friday night. Seduction 101. Either they would spend the night together or not. And if they didn't, James wasn't sure what would happen after that. He didn't want to think about the possibilities either.

Chapter 6

James was on his way to pick up Grace. They were attending a Leaders In Education gala at The Montpelier Hotel, a couple of hours away from the city. Though James was a former educator, he remained current on his certification. He had also built relationships with administrators that he still maintained. He received the invitation months ago and decided to attend, after Grace agreed to go with him. The event was at a hotel: check one. It was far enough away from people that would know them: check two. They would be together and closer than ever: check three. All the odds were in his favor, especially since Grace hadn't kicked him to the curb yet.

James planned out everything. He had much more in store for her beyond dinner. He was excited about their evening out… and their planned extra-curricular activities later on. The thought brought more than a smile to his face as he knocked on Grace's apartment door.

James was whistling a tune to himself when she opened

the door, but the sight of her caused him to fade out immediately.

"Hello," she greeted warmly.

"Hey… Nylah," he said, gazing at her from head to toe, back to head again.

Grace stepped aside for him to come in and as soon as the door closed, he pulled her into a sensual embrace and held her.

"You are gorgeous," he whispered, sliding his hand up and down the small of her back.

Rarely was he so taken with a woman, especially one not like he would normally choose. Change had proven to be good. James couldn't resist bending down to kiss her, just barely intensifying before pulling away. He carefully noted her response, pleased that she seemed to want more. *Just a little while longer…*

"You clean up nicely yourself, Mr. Garrison."

"You, uh… are you ready?" he asked, clearing his throat.

"Yes. I'm really excited, James. I hope you plan to make it worth my while," she smiled, teasing him.

"I don't think you'll be disappointed," he assured her. *You just wait, sweetheart. I'm about to change your life.*

****

James drove them to the hotel, the sounds of smooth jazz filling the car. When they arrived, Grace waited while he spoke with the hotel manager. They were then escorted to the ballroom where the gala was being held. As they were waiting to be seated, Grace drew closer to James, allowing him to wrap his arm around her waist affectionately.

"Mr. and Mrs. Garrison?" the hostess asked.

James nodded, feeling Grace tense up and inquire at him with her eyes. His eyes returned a response that implied they would talk at the table.

"Follow me, please," the hostess said, oblivious to their silent exchange.

James took Grace's hand and they were seated at their

table. As soon as she was out of earshot, James turned to face Grace, who was glaring at him.

"Why is she calling us Mr. and Mrs., James?"

"I may have neglected to mention on the response card that we weren't married. Does that bother you?" James asked.

"Yes, it bothers me. It feels…"

"Marital? Uncomfortable? Deceptive?" If he said it first, maybe she wouldn't be mad at his straightforward honesty.

"Yes, all of those things. But it also feels—" she paused before continuing, slight embarrassment creeping into her voice, "It feels kind of interesting."

He smiled broadly. "Interesting, huh? How so?"

"I don't know, mysterious maybe. Nobody knows we're not married except for us. That's kind of neat."

"Are you all right with others referencing me as your husband?" he asked, moving closer to her.

"I guess I can be all right with it for now," she assured, leaning into him. She briefly paused before kissing him lightly. "Does it make you uncomfortable for people to address me as your wife?"

"Not at all." James easily pulled Grace's chair closer to him to create an intimate closeness. He lightly grazed the top of her thighs as he carefully contemplated the wording in his next question. "Is it all right for me to treat you accordingly? You know, as a husband would treat his wife?"

Grace caught a suggestive hint in his tone, one that intrigued her curiosity. "Did you have something particular in mind?"

"Perhaps. I just want to know my boundaries—in that regard."

"When have you ever been concerned about boundaries?" Grace laughed as James feigned shock. "Do as you please, within good taste."

James smiled approvingly. This was going to be an outstanding night.

More people had begun to arrive at their table. They all soon became acquainted with one another. Grace and James were careful not to divulge any of their relationship details unless someone asked them, and even then, they were cautious with how they answered. Luckily, no one asked anything too personal.

Grace found herself comfortable in the role of James' "wife." During the 'meet and greet' they held hands, making their way around the ballroom. James encountered a few former colleagues, and introduced them to his companion Nylah. As they continued to mingle, he had no issue with holding her waist in a "husbandly way."

Throughout the night, they gave each other little kisses, or would show affection in other ways. Into the evening James had started calling her different terms of endearment, and Grace found herself loving every moment. After awhile, it didn't feel so imaginary. They were really acting like a married couple. Grace knew she should not let this continue—she even felt a twinge of guilt. But, she could not deny the warm feeling swirling around her insides either. Or maybe she just didn't want to.

As the evening wound to a close, James felt good about his chances. They had easily settled into the 'married couple' role. Almost too comfortably so… but he could think about that later. He watched Grace as she talked to another woman at the table, but he was soon lost in his own thoughts about the time they would spend together later on.

"James… James… Yoohoooo!" Grace called out in a singsong voice.

James hadn't even noticed Grace trying to get his attention until she shook him.

He snapped out of his thoughts to find Grace smiling at him.

"Are you back?" she grinned.

"Oh, yeah. Just thinking about some stuff."

"Well, can you think about it somewhere else? Everyone

is starting to leave."

James glanced around to see that the ballroom was indeed less than half full. He turned back to Grace, his anticipation rising. It was now or never.

"Uh yeah, we can go. You ready?"

Grace nodded and he took her hand and led her out into the lobby.

"Excuse me, sweetheart. I'll be right back." He wanted to double check with the hotel manager to make sure everything was in place.

The manager assured him that every detail had been taken care of and he even threw in a few extra special bonuses. James thanked him and returned to where he had left Grace.

Grace smiled at him, feeling a bit flirtatious in her manner. He smiled back at her, increasing the warmth she already felt throughout her body. When she asked if he was now ready, he leaned into her and kissed her with what Grace felt was a not-so-subtle hint of desire.

"I want to show you something, okay?"

Grace eyed him carefully and let him lead her to the elevators. Once inside and alone, he wrapped his arms around her and kissed her just behind her ear.

"Where are we going?" she asked him quietly.

"It's a surprise," he whispered in her ear. He held her close and took in her scent.

Grace closed her eyes and held him tighter, partially to keep her balance. The way he was holding her seemed to have a dizzying effect on her. They rode up, uninterrupted, coming to a stop at the top floor. James led her down the hall to a corner room at the end.

"We get to see one of the rooms?" Grace inquired.

"Something like that." James took out a key and smiled at Grace just before opening the door.

Grace entered the room, James right behind her. He turned on the entry light, so she could see into the rest of the room. As she stepped further in, James carefully gauged her body language and reaction. He heard her take in a sharp gasp and waited for her response.

Grace absorbed the room with wide-eyed examination, her mouth slightly gaped. There were lit candles, strategically placed around the room. There was soft music playing in the background, snacks around the wet bar, two overnight bags on the floor… and a bed with downturned covers, beckoning them.

Oh, no… Grace knew she brought this on herself. She stopped trying to fight James' advances a while ago, but maybe she didn't think it would have come to this. She was hoping that it wouldn't, because although she knew what she had to do, she didn't think she was, or wanted to be, strong enough to resist him.

James came up behind her, circling her waist with his arm. Grace took his hand, stepped out of his embrace and turned to face him. She contemplated for a few seconds before speaking.

"What's all this?" she asked as lightly as she could.

James wasn't fooled. She was definitely affected, but he wasn't sure in what regard. "This is for you."

"And for you?" she asked, her brow slightly raised.

"For us," he answered.

"Why?" she whispered, trying to fight back tears.

James slowly closed the distance between them. He held her in his arms and gave her an effortless, pleasant kiss. He pulled back just a little and bore his gaze into her glistening eyes.

"I seem to have spent the past few weeks falling in love with you," he started. "I didn't plan for that to happen, but I'm glad it did."

"Really?" Grace asked.

James nodded. Grace had no idea his declaration would affect her so deeply. She closed her eyes and felt a few tears fall down her cheeks. She opened them again and hesitated.

"I love you too, James." Grace reached up slowly and

initiated the kiss, but allowed James to take over and he did not disappoint. He broke away right at the brink of intensity.

"I want to be completely yours... here, tonight. If you'll have me," James uttered.

There it was. Now the choice was hers.

Grace paused again. "We shouldn't be here. Not for this... not like this. It's not right."

"I won't disagree with you. We are both adults, so it must be our mutual decision. If you want to leave we can go right now and I'll take you home." To emphasize his point, he released her and stepped back.

Grace immediately felt herself frowning at his distance. She wanted to be close to him. She wanted to be *this* close to him. He was providing her with the opportunity to make the right choice... the choice she knew she needed to make, and yet... she didn't move. He had presented her with two options: either grab their things and leave, or accept his very indecent, yet tantalizing proposal. Every part of her conscience screamed at her to run for the door. Every part of her flesh burned with an intense desire to stay the night with him.

Grace had never been so torn in her life. She was supposed to be the good girl. She had never been with a man before... James knew that. And this was not the way she envisioned her first time. She was supposed to be married before this happened. *What's happened to me?* But she already knew the answer. She had compromised herself a long time ago... when she went back to James after their first encounter. That decision enabled her to be here with him now, considering his seductive proposal.

Grace wandered to the window, watching the lights illuminate the city. She sighed and wiped the tears that were falling. James came to her and wrapped his arms around her, the way she loved.

"Are you okay?" he asked.

Grace leaned back into him and held onto him. "Probably

not."

"Do you want to leave?"

The tears streamed faster. "No..."

"Do you want to stay?"

Grace nodded, but that wasn't enough for James; he needed to hear her say the words. He gently turned her around to face him and repeated his question. "Do you want to stay?"

Grace's sobs shook her body. She couldn't directly face him. Not yet. With her eyes closed, she quietly answered him through her sobs. "Yes. I want to stay."

James pulled her close and held her until her emotions calmed. Then he lifted her head and gave her long, slow kisses, easing the tension away. He pulled back once more.

"Are you sure?" he asked.

Grace peered at him, finally. "Yes," she sniffled. "But I'm nervous... and scared."

"Don't worry. I promised to take care of you, didn't I?"

Grace nodded and they embraced. "I trust you," she whispered.

James internalized her words, realizing how long it had been since a woman extended her trust to him. He kissed her for a long time before he led her to the bed.

****

Grace was not able to sleep. The reality of what she and James had done began to sink in. She slid out of bed, put on a robe and sat by the window, observing the morning's sunrise. She couldn't stop the fresh round of tears that overtook her after James fell asleep.

What have I done? Why have I allowed this to happen? What's going to happen next? Grace was so weighed down with heavy thoughts, but she had no one to blame but herself. She may have been inexperienced, but she wasn't stupid. She knew that James had wanted to sleep with her after their first encounter. You don't make out with someone like that without something else in mind. *But would this be it? Would he take her home and act like it never happened?* Grace knew that should be the furthest thought from her mind. She needed to think about the spiritual consequences, but she didn't think she could take that along with the possibility of James' rejection. She sat and cried for a little while, not realizing that James had woken up and was watching her.

James wondered what was wrong with Grace. *Had he hurt her? Did she regret their night? Was she going to tell him that it was a mistake and she didn't want to be with him anymore?* All of those thoughts brought a frown to his face. He was hoping she wouldn't reject him now. Not after the night they just had. He knew she had been fighting her conscience more than he allowed himself to fight with his. Maybe that's what was wrong. Either way, he intended to find out. He got out of bed, slid into a pair of pants, and approached her. He swung his leg around and sat behind her, so she could lean back against him. He wasn't sure how to interpret her demeanor.

"What's the matter?" he asked.

"I don't know if I want to talk about it right now."

"Okay. But I can tell you're worried about something," he coaxed.

"How can you tell? I could just be emotionally unstable," she replied in a matter of fact tone.

James chuckled. "Not a chance. I know you, Grace. You're not unstable, you're upset."

Grace partially turned to glance at him briefly before leaning back against him again.

"You rarely call me Grace."

"I know," he said smiling. "I'm trying it out."

Grace thoughtfully traced a pattern on his pants. "I like that you call me Nylah," she said after awhile. "Everybody calls me Grace, but you're the only one who calls me Nylah. I'd prefer if you keep it that way."

James saw hints of a smile, judging by the way her cheekbones went up. "Okay, then. Nylah, it is." He kissed the inside of her palm affectionately. "I, uhhh, I didn't hurt you did I?" James asked hesitantly.

Grace turned to him, eyes wide. "No, no. Is that why you think I'm crying?"

"Not really, but it did cross my mind. I just wanted to make sure."

"Believe me; you did not hurt me at all. If anything, you..." Grace's voiced trailed off, not wanting to verbalize how tempted she was to stay in bed with him.

They sat quiet before Grace spoke again. "James... this isn't... like, you won't... I mean we..." Grace didn't know how to ask him.

James sensed she wanted some reassurance. "You know, when I first saw you crying, I was so scared that you were going to reject me that I never considered you might be afraid of the very same thing."

"Why are you scared of my rejection?" Grace asked.

"Because... you know what happened with Janelle. I've never opened my heart to any other woman until you. I wasn't kidding when I said that I love you. That's real. Being abandoned is not something I care to experience again, but I thought your remorse would drive you to decide that it's best if we don't communicate anymore."

Grace covered his hand with hers, understanding that their individual fear of rejection seemed to bond them closer.

"I was scared that you would just toss me aside and act like this never happened," Grace confided.

"Sweetheart, I would never do that to you. What we shared was real... more real than I could have ever imagined. And it means a lot that you have trusted me with your feelings... and your body."

Grace felt her insides warming up again, but she needed to fan the flames for now.

"James, this doesn't take away from the fact that what we're doing—it's wrong."

James stared hard at her. "Yes, I know. We both know that it's wrong."

"And that doesn't bother you? How can you be so insensitive about it? Like it doesn't matter."

"Look Nylah, I've done my battle with it. Frankly, I made up my mind a long time ago. I have to deal with that in my own way. It also doesn't change the fact that you knew it was wrong, but you stayed anyway."

Grace drew in a sharp breath and slowly stood up. Her voice was sharp, her eyes blazing. "You know, you're right. I did choose to stay, so I guess that makes me no better than you. But I did not take time to make plans and think through the proper channels of seduction. You've spent a lot of time thinking about this, haven't you? Was this your goal from the very beginning? To get me into bed? So much for your whole 'you work really hard and I just want to show you how much I appreciate it' speech."

James cringed. She was right…and she finally called him on it. He couldn't deny it. But if she thought that was all this was about, he would have to convince her that his feelings were real.

"Yes, I admit…I did seek you out for this purpose. But that was in the beginning. I told you last night that I didn't plan on falling in love with you, but I'm glad I did."

Grace softened a little. Then she changed, just like that. "Of course, you would say that. Anything to make me feel better about having sex with you."

"Would you stop it? My being in love with you has nothing to do with sex."

"Right. Because you would have had sex with me regardless."

James tried to keep calm, but he was becoming as irritated as she was upset. *What was going on?* "This is not about sex right now."

"Are you serious? Did we not just spend hours involved in that very activity?"

James approached her, stopping just in front of her. "Yes, we did. And you liked it. No… you *loved* it. Dare I say that you want it to happen again, but you want to make me feel bad because it's wrong."

Grace flushed, trying to keep her emotions in check... all of them. She was finding it rather difficult for a few of them with James standing so close to her. "The both of us should feel bad enough to not do it again! It goes against everything that is morally right."

"Yes... the both of us should feel bad enough. Which raises the question: do you feel bad enough—to not do it again?"

Grace started to answer him, but couldn't make a sound. She was railing at him about their morals and she couldn't even say that she would do what was right.

"Are you going to answer me?" he asked. He traced her jaw line with his finger, moving down her neck to her shoulder.

Grace shook her head no, scared to move an inch beyond that. She felt an instant spark at his touch and a shiver ran down her spine.

"James, please stop. Move... away... please."

"Only if you drop this conversation. I don't want to talk about it anymore today."

"I'll drop it for now. But we're not finished with it."

"We'll never be finished with it, sweetheart."

She thought about his statement as he stepped back. "Why do you—"

A knock interrupted her question. James went to answer, returning with a breakfast cart. He asked her if she was hungry, but she didn't answer. She was really hungry, but she didn't think she could eat anything. She didn't know what to say to him and the silence swirling around them felt like it was going to suffocate her. What made it worse was that the air was charged with varying levels of uncomfortable, and still sensual, tension.

On the ride home, Grace could barely come up with two words to say. Her emotions were in turmoil; she had plenty of thoughts to sort through. James tried to talk to her, but she only gave him short answers. He gave up in frustration after she just finally asked him to leave her alone. They rode the rest of the way in irritated silence.

Once they reached her apartment, Grace tried to tell him he didn't need to help her up, but he insisted. She tried to object again, but this time she gave up after he pinned her with a scathing glare. She was trying to avoid letting him into her apartment, mainly because she was afraid that he wouldn't leave until the next morning. She knew she couldn't resist him for long no matter how upset or irritated she was with him.

"I got it. You can go now," she urged.

"Just open the door, Nylah," he said.

Grace sighed heavily before turning the knob and letting him in.

"Don't worry, I'm not going to stay."

His declaration affected her, but she didn't want to let him see that.

"Well, thank you... for..." she began.

"Don't. You don't have to thank me for anything. I'll see you tomorrow." Then he turned and left. No hug, no kiss—nothing.

Grace was kind of hurt at his briskness, but she hadn't given him much choice. She watched him leave, wanting to call out to him, but not allowing herself to. Once he closed the door, she felt another round of tears begin to fall.

The battle was in her mind. *I don't want to spend tonight without him. Having a wrong relationship with James is not worth destroying my relationship with God. He loves me... and I love him too. If he really loved me, he would not have propositioned me in a hotel room. If I really loved God, I would not have allowed myself to stay with him in that room. This is not his fault... I'm to blame completely for my part. Why is this happening?* Grace cried off and on for the rest of the night, wrestling with her thoughts. She didn't sleep well, upset that she was in limbo between feeling a heavy spiritual guilt and sadness about James not being there with her. *Seriously... what have I done?*

****

The next morning, Grace felt overheated, nauseous and somewhat lightheaded while she was getting ready for church. She breathlessly kept pausing to fan herself with her hand, or anything she could find that could bring her at least a semblance of relief. This was far worse than after their first encounter. She was trying to be the voice of reason, but she couldn't reason the fact that she didn't completely regret sleeping with him. She took her time getting ready, dreading her inevitable encounter with James at church.

****

Church was torture for Grace, finding herself an emotional mess during service. She had arrived late, namely to avoid James, sitting in the back, making every effort to not glance his way. She knew Dani would be searching for her, so she was sure to sit near an exit to make a quick getaway after service.

Grace was mildly surprised that James didn't preach that morning; Lawrence did. Grace knew she should go to the altar—she had some serious repenting to do. Her only problem was that she couldn't budge. She had willingly slept with James and didn't want to spend time apologizing if she were just going to do it again, which was where her desires were. None of this was right. What was she going to do? What was she thinking getting involved with him? She sat and struggled with her thoughts right up until the benediction. That's when she dashed out of the side door.

****

James was a wreck on the inside. Not for reasons he should have been, but for reasons concerning Grace. He didn't like the way he left her yesterday afternoon. It stressed him to leave her apartment that way. Yesterday had been emotionally charged. He had been with women before, but this was different—unlike any other situation he had ever been in. He hadn't expected to want her this much. He was going to have to find a way to resolve how their relationship would survive. James watched as he saw Grace leave in a hurry. She had come in late and sat on the back pew. She was avoiding him again. This time, he would put a stop to it.

****

That evening, Grace was reorganizing the books on her bookshelf. She was trying to occupy her mind and time with busy work, but nothing helped. Dani had called her four times, and each call, Grace ignored. Grace eventually sent Dani a text, which hopefully pacified her. All of the other phone calls she received were also ignored. She wasn't ready to face anyone yet.

But James had not called her. Grace wasn't sure how she felt about that. When someone knocked on her door, she approached, not wanting to answer. It was going to be at least one of three people because no one else ever came to her apartment.

"Who is it?" she called out.

"It's James."

Shoot! What is he doing here? Grace took in a few deep breaths and opened the door.

"Hello," she greeted.

"Can I come in?"

James seemed mostly relaxed, but she could tell something was on his mind. Grace nodded and stepped aside to let him in. She closed and locked the door and moved past him when he stopped her. Pulling her to him, he held her waist and gazed at her.

"This is how I prefer to greet you," he said before sweeping her into a kiss.

Grace more than willingly complied, making no effort to stop him. She savored the feeling of being connected to him. After he pulled away, Grace re-gathered her composure, trying to focus her train of thought.

"Why… are you here?" she asked.

He sat on the couch. "You were late to church this morning."

Grace started to interrupt him, but he held up his hand to stop her. "Then, you didn't come back to service tonight. You are doing your best to avoid me and I would like to know why."

Grace sighed and sat next to him. She couldn't resist touching him any longer. She stroked the back of his head as he pulled her closer, holding her waist. "I've been having a great deal of trouble processing what happened between us. On top of that, how am I supposed to face people knowing I just spent the night with our pastor? That is very uncomfortable for me."

"Do you regret staying with me?" James asked.

Grace's eyes watered. "I know that I should, but... but, I don't. And that's what contributes to my mental struggle. It is very conflicting."

"I am sorry that I have put you in this position. I didn't think past what I wanted, to how this would affect you."

"I can't blame you for my choice. I just need to figure out how to deal with all these emotions."

They sat for a few moments in contemplative silence.

"James. What's going to happen now?"

James studied her. "I want to be with you. Hopefully you will oblige me in a mutual relationship."

"Like in a sexual relationship? You want us to be lovers?"

"Not just sex. I want us to be *together*. I'm just not ready for marriage."

Grace paused, pondering his last statement. "You... don't want... to marry me?" she slowly asked. "Or—"

James stopped her with a kiss. "My thoughts about marriage have nothing to do with you. And if my feelings ever change about it, believe me, you will be the first to know."

His explanation caused Grace some relief. Still, how did she feel about engaging in a full-fledged affair with James?

That was a lot different from just spending one night together.

"James, we won't be able to tell anyone about our relationship. It will have to remain a secret."

"I have no problems with that. I prefer privacy."

"What if something happens? Or what if we meet other people? And what about—what about using protection?"

James frowned at her. "First, I'm telling you now; I have no intention of meeting anybody else."

Grace smiled. She didn't want anybody else either.

"Second, I will purchase the protection for us to use. And finally, if something happens," he continued, "we'll just deal with it as it comes."

"So…"

"So what?" James said, bringing her to him for a probing kiss.

"What about Dani and Lawrence?" Grace managed to ask.

"We'll handle them," James said, intensifying their kiss. He ran his hand up her thigh and settled it on her hip. Grace sighed and leaned into him further.

"I was devastated when you left yesterday," Grace whispered, brushing her fingers across his lips. "I know I was being difficult and I'm sorry. But I didn't want you to leave."

"I was equally devastated to leave you," he said while exploring her with his eyes and hands. "Especially like that. If you had stopped me, I would have stayed until this morning. I happen to like being here with you."

"That's what I was afraid of and I didn't know how to handle that. Because I like you being here with me, too. But since you're here now, you can stay… until…"

James stopped what he was doing. A slow smile spread across his face.

"Is that a yes… to my request? You'll be with me?"

Grace held the side of his face. "It's wrong. It's so wrong."

"I know, baby. I know it is," he said, pulling her beneath him.

"I love you so much," she said to him.

"I love you, too," he whispered to her as he brought her to a place where she could let go. After a while, he carried her to her bedroom and stayed until morning.

Chapter 7

Grace and James exchanged keys to each other's homes. Over the next several months, they practically lived together, alternating weeks spent at each other's homes. They learned as much about the other as possible, learning each other's temperaments and each other's dreams. They took short trips together whenever they could. They also took turns trying out their opposite interests.

Grace lavished James with as much love, attention and affection as possible, without being overbearing. She was able to personally and intimately see, hear, and feel the pain James' divorce had caused him. She could see that every day they were together was a process of inner healing for him. As that weight steadily lifted, Grace noticed the emotional and mental change in him.

James, for his part, tended to Grace's every need and desire. Grace had to admit she was rather spoiled. James gave her whatever she wanted and he loved her fiercely. He took pride in the fact that Grace loved him for the person he was.

Their interactions were easy and natural, but they remained cautious about being together in public. One Sunday after evening service, the members were standing around talking, preparing to leave. James stopped Grace as she passed by his car. He leaned in to her, but not too close to cause suspicion and said, "I'll see you at home." They were spending this particular week at his house. "Oh... and leave the dress on," he said with a spark in his eyes.

Mortified that he would say something provocative to her on church grounds, Grace hoped no one noticed their personal exchange. She didn't respond, she only glared at him and left in a flustered huff.

When James got home, Grace was already spoiling for a fight.

"Why would you say something like that to me? *At church! That was beyond inappropriate, James!"*

"Sweetheart, our entire relationship is beyond inappropriate," James shot back.

"Wait, am I speaking to James or to Pastor Garrison right now? I've had trouble deciphering the two for months. Because I mean really, who else has a pastor that asks his secretary to have a sexual relationship with him? I wonder how I got to be the lucky one!"

"Spare me the righteous indignation, Grace. Don't play yourself." He moved toward her with purpose. "You knew what I wanted before I asked you... and you still said yes," he said, backing her into the wall. His eyes were lit with a seductive fire as he grabbed her waist and added, "So, maybe I should ask how *I* got to be the lucky one."

Grace's breathing quickened. It never failed to happen when James touched her.

"James, move. We're having a discussion."

James bent down to kiss a trail up her neck. "No, you want to have a fight. I'm done with it," he murmured against her throat. "If you want to continue, don't let me stop you." He moved to kiss her at one of her most sensitive spots.

"I am... trying to be angry with you. How do you expect me to continue..." Grace sighed, all of her ire melting away, "when you do that?"

James kissed her with an evident desire for immediate gratification. Pulling away he said, "You can always tell me to stop."

"Not that you would," Grace managed, gripping James and pulling him closer.

"Not that you want me to," James whispered in her ear.

Grace clearly knew that she had lost, which she knew was James' intention from the very beginning. *I am so easy.* "You know I can't resist you." *I don't want to resist you...*

"Then you'll be glad to know the feeling is mutual," he said.

They eventually ended up in bed, cooling down.

"Someone's becoming rather uninhibited, huh?" James teased. He laced his fingers through hers and wrapped himself around her.

Grace blushed bashfully. "I don't know what happened."

"Well, whatever it was, it can happen anytime you want," James nuzzled against her neck. He whispered in her ear, and grinned when he saw an even deeper red settle in her cheeks. By night's end, it had turned out to be an evening of new experiences for them both.

****

Despite Grace's assurance, Nathan seemed to still pose a threat to James. She knew James had seen her talking to Nathan at church one Wednesday evening. He ardently expressed to her later on his desire for them to not be so friendly anymore.

"You're being rather attentive, James. Are you all right?"

James contemplated her question, but he didn't answer.

Grace sat up and continued. "You've been quiet since we left my apartment. Once we got here, you were *very* engaged—to say the least. What's going on?"

James wasn't sure if she had picked up on his mood. He

had obviously done a poor job in hiding his feelings. Sitting up, he decided the direct approach would be best.

"I don't like you talking to Nathan. I can't stand it. It makes me feel outrageously jealous and I don't know how to handle that," James told her.

Grace sighed. She thought they had been over this already. "James, I already told you Nathan and I are just friends. There is nothing going on. I don't have feelings for him beyond friendship."

"It's not so much about you; it's more about him. I don't trust him and I don't think he feels the same way you do. He likes you, Nylah."

"Why do you think so?"

"I'm a man. I can tell when another man is feeling my lady, and as flattered as I could be that you're so desirable, I don't like him around you."

"I don't spend time with Nathan. You don't need to be jealous."

James stood and paced around the room. "Nylah, you're not listening to me. I don't like you talking to him. And I want you to stop."

Grace's eyes widened. This was a first for them.

"You want me to stop talking to one of my friends? Because you don't know how to handle your jealousy?" Grace was trying to proceed with caution because there were many different ways this conversation could go.

James stood across the room, glaring at her with a raised level of irritation. "Yes. I know that it sounds unreasonable, but that's how I feel."

"What if I say no?" Grace asked.

James was stricken with displeasure. "You would do that? Why?"

"James, that's a little more than unreasonable. And I'm not saying I would, I'm just asking 'what if?'"

Shrugging, James turned away. "I don't know."

He really has a problem with this. Well, if he's making requests, I can make one too. "James are you willing to do a fair trade?"

"What are you talking about?" he gruffly asked her.

"I know that you must interact with the women at the church. You're the pastor. I get it. Just... be careful."

Raising a brow and not fooled by her generalized statement, he pressed her for more information. "Anyone in particular I should be concerned about?"

Pausing, Grace realized that maybe this bothered her more than she was willing to acknowledge. "Yes. Valencia."

"Reynolds? I don't even talk to her. I try not to if I can manage."

"Exactly. Which means that she seeks you out. Why? Because she likes you. You don't need to be around her."

"Are you perhaps jealous of her?" James teased.

"Not at all. But her constant presence around you is irritating. And she's just the most forward. Women throw themselves at you all the time. It's not easy to watch." Grace had to make sure she remained calm. *Is this what he feels like?*

"Why are you just now saying something about this?"

"Why would I bring it up, James? This all seems so silly!"

They both remained silent for a few minutes. Finally, James asked, "If Nathan were to ask you out, would you go?"

"Like on a date? NO! Do you honestly think I would do that to you?" Grace asked.

James sat on the bed, his back facing Grace. He sighed slowly. "No. I don't think you would." There were so many thoughts racing through his head, but Grace managed to touch on the most sensitive one.

"I'm not Janelle. You cannot attach what she did to you, to me. I'm not going to leave you for another man, James. I'm not."

Sighing heavily, James nodded. "I know. I'm sorry. I guess I could have asked you to stop talking to Nathan instead of telling you."

Grace eased up behind him and wrapped her arms around him. "If you really want me to stop talking to him, I will. But

I need you to agree to be careful. And if you know a woman is flirting with you, I need you to shut it down."

Pulling her around to sit on his lap, he said, "Done. You won't have anything to worry about. Does this mean that we're not going to see other people?"

"Do you really have to ask? I thought we were exclusive from the very beginning," Grace said.

Pulling her in for a kiss, he said, "I just wanted to affirm that you're mine."

Returning his kiss, she whispered, "Yep. I'm all yours."

James had pulled back rather significantly from ministering. He still did all the things his position dictated, but on a much smaller scale. Lawrence, and the other Elders and Ministers slowly and steadily acquired more responsibility. At first, he and Grace had decided that they wouldn't spend the night together, prior to Bible class and Sundays, but that soon became history. They just could not stay away from each other.

James often found himself thinking of Grace as his wife. He treated her as such whenever he could and she reciprocated in kind. They shared trusts, confidence and love. But their relationship was marked.

They were living in sin every single day and they fought about it all the time. As much and as hard as they loved, they fought. Grace was consistent in verbalizing their predicament... but oddly, never enough to leave him. He had certainly never given thought to ending their relationship. But fighting was no use. Even if they stayed upset with each other, they always came together eventually. However, they both knew that what they had could not, and would not, continue this way forever. Something needed to happen. They needed to make it as right as they could.

Chapter 8

Grace was waiting for James in their hotel suite. They had decided to meet up for a mini vacation to celebrate her birthday. He had been out of town at a leadership conference, so she hadn't seen him all week, but they talked every day. They picked a mutual, out-of-state destination and planned accordingly. Instead of a chain hotel, he'd selected a high-end posh, local charmer with intimate appeal. Grace glanced at her watch. He was late; he'd called her earlier to tell her his flight was delayed. She hoped he would make it in time for their plans. She didn't know what they were going to do; James just told her how to dress.

While she waited for him, she decided to finish getting ready, humming as she went along. Then she stretched out across the luxuriously plush bed, thinking about earlier in the month when they had both been at Lawrence and Dani's house. Dani and Grace had been talking in private.

"So... Gracie, I've been thinking."
"Uh oh... About what?" Grace asked.

"Well, you and James seem to be growing closer in general. Have you ever considered going out to dinner with him?"

Grace smiled. "James is nice and we have a good working relationship, but I'm not his type."

"You never know. He might be interested," Dani hinted.

Grace's heart fluttered. "You didn't say anything to him did you?"

Dani appeared contrite. "No, but Lawrence did."

"Dani!"

"I know. I know you don't like that and I'm sorry, but we couldn't help it. He needs a good woman and you would be a good fit for him. Besides, he didn't reject the idea. He seemed kind of interested, actually."

Grace was quiet. She had to play along with Dani, but she was amused. "Really? He seemed interested?"

Dani nodded, smiling.

"Why did Lawrence decide to ask him?"

"You remember that one Sunday when I kept calling you? Finally, you sent me a text that you were sick and that's why I hadn't seen you at church."

Grace nodded, swallowing a lump in her throat. That was the Sunday after.

"Well, I wanted to check on you, but I had promised Lawrence we would spend the evening together, uninterrupted. James volunteered with a promise to update us after he saw you. He seemed really concerned and we thought it was sweet. That's when we thought about you two being together. Or, at least exploring the possibility. What do you think?"

What do I think? We've been together for months and have done plenty of exploring. And thank goodness you didn't come by that night... or the rest of the week. Grace sighed. Their friends were trying to play matchmaker. She did feel a little guilty though. Dani would be more than hurt if she ever found out about her and James keeping their relationship a secret.

"Well, I guess I'll have to talk to James, but he has to bring it up. Otherwise it won't be discussed."

"We already knew that, so don't worry. I'm sure he'll be talking to you later."

Grace eyed Dani's grin. As they continued talking, the guys interrupted them.

"Nylah, can I talk to you for a few minutes... in private?" James asked.

Dani flew to Lawrence's side, the both of them smiling broadly. *"I think that's a good idea,"* she encouraged. *"We'll stay here. You can talk in our study."*

James locked the door behind them after they entered the room. He sat next to Grace and grinned slyly at her. She returned with a laugh as he pulled her into a needy kiss. After a few minutes, they pulled away, breathless and ready to leave.

"So, how about them trying to hook us up?" Grace asked, relaxing in his embrace.

"I know. It seems like a pretty good idea. Lucky for us, I thought of it first. I suppose it's no problem for us to play along."

"Does that mean we can leave to 'spend more time together'?"

James caught her meaning. *"Don't worry. I'll get us out of here in five minutes."*

He hadn't been playing. In five minutes flat, Grace was driving off in her car, James right behind her. They went back to his house for the rest of that week.

Grace snapped back to the present when she heard a key in the hotel door. She heard the door close and a deep voice call out to her.

"Nylah! Baby, are you in here?"

Grace got up as quick as she could and went to him, grinning all the way. "You're here!" she said running into his arms.

James wrapped his arms around her tightly. He had missed her. "I'm so happy to see you. Happy Birthday, baby," he whispered in her ear.

"I love you," she cooed to him. He pulled her back and inundated her with kisses so pleasurable she thought they would have to cancel their plans and stay in.

"You really did miss me, huh?" she asked.

He kissed her again in response.

"Mmmm... I missed you, too," she murmured against his lips. "And if you don't stop kissing me, I just might have to show you how much."

She could feel the effects her words had on him.

"I'm not totally against that idea," he smiled, "but perhaps we should wait until later. I would hate to spoil the plans I made specifically for you tonight. I think you're going to love it."

"Awww James, I'm so excited. What are we doing? Where are we going? Are you going to tell me now?"

"Sssshhh. Patience, sweetheart... you'll see soon enough." With that, he stepped back to let his eyes slowly graze over her and let out an appreciative whistle. He came back to her and affirmed, "I also have special plans for you when we get back."

James' voice was thick with heated desire, making Grace weak all over. She sighed against him, urging him to hurry so they could be on their way.

****

A few hours later, they returned to their room. Grace felt like she was floating on air. James led her to the room and encouraged her to relax on the bed while he went to get a few things for her.

Grace reflected on their evening. He had arranged for car service to take them to a dinner theatre. Grace enjoyed the food, but she really enjoyed the show; she loved that type of thing. From there, they strolled a short distance in the breezy night air to the harbor. They took a moonlight cruise around the marina on a private yacht. There were two musicians on board: a trumpet, and an acoustic guitar player, personnel for proper boat operation, and an attendant to check on them periodically. Once they had settled in, James observed a glowing Grace.

"You did all this for me?" she asked, touched by his thoughtfulness.

James pulled her close and whispered to her all the things he would do for her. He told her how much he loved her, he told her what he loved about her and he told her why he would love her forever. They rode in content silence, listening to the soothing sounds of their live music, occasionally commenting on something they saw, but not needing to speak many words.

Grace came out of her thoughts and noticed James had not yet returned.

"What are you doing?" she called out.

"I'm coming!" he called back. After a few more moments, he appeared at the door with a few bags and boxes. "I come bearing gifts," he said, handing Grace most of what was in his hands.

"All these are mine?" she asked, her eyes dancing with anticipation.

"All for you," he assured her.

Grace eagerly opened each item. There were nine gifts total, each one holding a special meaning for her.

"Wait, one's missing," James muttered, searching for the other gift. "There's supposed to be ten." He scanned his bag, but he didn't find it. "Ah...I know where it is." He went to his suitcase and rummaged briefly before pulling out another small gift box. "Ten," he declared, returning to Grace. He took her hand and turned her to sit up on the edge of the bed. He handed her the box.

"Open it," he encouraged.

"Ooooo... what is it?" Grace asked curiously.

"Open it," he said again, squatting down in front of her.

Grace pulled the ribbon and lifted the lid off the top. She pulled out a small jewelry box. Judging from its size, she knew that it could only hold one of very few things... and her ears weren't pierced. *Could it be?* She held the box and travelled her gaze to James, who had repositioned himself to one knee.

"James," she whispered.

"Are you going to open it?" he asked gently.

"Not yet. What is it?" She was still whispering; her voice seemed to have given out on her.

"I would rather you open it and find out."

The tears seemed to pool around in her eyes, teasing a waterfall. She took a deep breath and opened the box. It glistened a gorgeous sparkle. She gasped and the tears fell. James smiled.

"See, I've been thinking," he started. "When we go out, we're Mr. and Mrs. Garrison. When we're at home, we're acting in every way, like husband and wife. I've tried to fight it, telling myself that I wasn't ready for marriage again, but when I'm away from you, I think about you all the time. I think about wanting to be with you, wanting you to be the mother of my children and ... wanting you to be my wife. We've been acting married for so long; I sometimes forget that we're not. It's time to rectify that. Please forgive me... I should have married you a long time ago and I'm sorry I didn't."

"You don't have to apologize to me. It's done. And it was our choice to do it."

James took the box from Grace and removed the ring.

"It's gorgeous," she said.

"It doesn't do you justice," he replied.

Grace smiled at him as he kissed her hands.

"Nylah, I love you more than I ever thought I could love a woman. You taught me how to trust again. You made it okay for me to open up to you and give you my heart. I know we haven't been right, but I want to make us as right as possible. I want to marry you. I want you to marry me. I want us to have a family."

"I want all of those things too," she softly assured him. "And I want them with you."

James' jaw clenched. He hadn't expected to feel so

emotional. He took a deep breath. Gazing into her eyes made it so much easier to ask her. "Nylah Grace Anderson, it has been my privilege to love you. Will you do me the honor of becoming my wife and let me love you forever?"

Grace smiled as big as she could. "Yes. Yes, I would love to be your wife. And yes, I promise to love you forever."

James slid the ring on her finger and kissed her. During a moment of rest sometime in the night, they were both in the same thought: if marriage turned out to be better than this, they couldn't believe their good fortune.

Chapter 9

Two weekends later, Grace and James went over to Dani and Lawrence's house for lunch. Although no one else knew about them being together now, James was able to be more affectionate with Grace when they were around their friends. Especially since Dani and Lawrence "hooked them up."

Grace had to remember to take her ring off, since their engagement was not public knowledge yet. After initial greetings, James kissed Grace on her cheek before she joined Dani to help her finish setting up for lunch on the patio.

"Soooo... how is everything?" Dani smiled.

"Everything is good," Grace answered, not giving Dani the information she desired.

"Just good?" Dani asked.

Grace knew she was subtly fishing, but Grace was not so easy in obliging. She just nodded and said, "Yeah. Good."

Dani gave her an exasperated sigh. "Gracie! You know what I mean. How is everything with you and James? You two seem to be getting closer."

Grace smiled, thinking about their engagement... that she couldn't tell Dani about yet. Then her smiled faltered as if she suddenly remembered something else. She recovered and said, "Everything is great with James. He's pretty wonderful."

Grace thought she had recovered from her slight falter. She hadn't recovered quick enough to escape Dani's notice though.

"What's wrong, Gracie? Are you okay? Is something wrong... with James?"

"No... no. It's me," Grace said. She had seemed to zone out for a minute, puzzling Dani.

"What about you, honey?" Dani asked.

"I don't know Dani. I—I may be in trouble." Grace wished she could tell Dani everything right then and there. She had never felt the urge to come clean so strong before now.

"What kind of trouble, Gracie?" When Grace didn't answer, Dani slightly nudged her. "Grace?"

Grace shook herself out of her spaced-out zone. "Huh?"

"You said you might be in trouble. What kind?"

Grace squeezed her eyes shut and took a few deep breaths. "It's nothing, Dani. Never mind."

"Gracie..." Dani started.

"Please, Dani. I know I said it, but I'm asking you to drop it."

"Is it bad? You know you can trust me, right?" Dani asked, trying not to express her growing concern.

Grace nodded. "Yes, I know that. It's not about you." Seeing the hurt in Dani's eyes, Grace tried to explain without explaining. "I wish I could tell you. I just can't right now. And I'm not even sure about it, so it's premature. When I know for certain, I'll tell you. Okay?"

Dani understood and she didn't pry anymore. Grace rarely kept anything from her, so the least she could do was give her space and the time she needed to get it all figured out.

After they ate, Dani cleared the table. Lawrence helped

her, leaving Grace and James outside.

"Baby, what's wrong?" James quietly asked her.

Grace was surprised at his question. She hadn't been acting different. "Why do you think something is wrong?"

"You're acting fine, but there is something in your eyes that indicates otherwise."

"I could just be tired. We've had some late nights..." Grace smiled.

"And some early mornings," James finished, matching her grin with one of his own. "But I've seen you tired. This isn't it, this is you internally worried. What is it?"

Grace shook her head slightly. "Ummm... Your observation surprises me."

"It shouldn't. We know each other well. And don't change the subject." He placed his arm around her and brought her a little closer. "What's on your mind?"

"James, the secrecy is killing me. I had managed to block it out for the most part, but it's getting worse."

James thought on her words. "It's actually been starting to get to me a bit, too. We can tell people we plan to get married. No one has to know about anything else."

"I want to tell people." Grace sighed, feeling something she couldn't pinpoint. "But not right now. Do you mind waiting?"

"No, I don't mind. You let me know when you're ready; then we can tell the world."

Grace smiled as he pulled her into a hug. Still holding her close, he said, "Once we make our announcement, I want to be married within six weeks."

"Okay. That's fine with me. I'll let you know when I'm ready."

Lawrence and Dani observed them talking from inside.

"I wonder why we didn't see this sooner. They do well together," Lawrence said.

"Yeah... they do," Dani slowly affirmed. "Lawrence, did you notice anything off about Grace?"

"She seemed a little withdrawn, maybe. People get like that sometimes. Why?"

"Something's going on with her. I'm not sure what, but I got a different feeling when she alluded to it."

"What are you thinking?"

"I don't know what to think. Grace has been pretty easy to figure mostly. But there have been a few times this year when I have had a strange feeling about her—"

"Strange how?" Lawrence asked.

"I don't know how to explain it. Like she may be in trouble of sorts, but I thought it was just me... until a little while ago, when we were talking. Now I know something is wrong, but she won't tell me what... yet. I'm really concerned about her."

"She'll tell you when she's ready. Until then, just pray for her and be the friend you've always been. Come on, let's go. They might start to get suspicious, like we're busy doing things married people do. We wouldn't want them to get any ideas."

"That's certainly not a good idea. Although, I think Grace would cringe at the thought."

****

"Kat, are you sure James and Lena haven't hooked up?"

Edward and Katherine were in their bedroom resting. They'd gone to breakfast that morning before going to the church for prayer and a few private meetings. They met Michelle, Rand and the girls for their weekly dinner before making their way back home.

Katherine paused reading to regard her husband. "Edward, I'm positive. Lena has been here. She doesn't have time for James, or for any other man. Besides, you asked him yourself."

"I just can't shake that he's up to something. But I know we won't find out unless it's exposed somehow."

"Maybe you should give him a little more credit."

"I can't say that he's earned that. He's crafty and

sometimes a little careless. You see the mess that happened with Janelle."

"How were any of us to know she would leave him like that?"

"He should not have married her. He takes over the church; she cheats on him, becomes pregnant with another man's baby, lies to him about it and leaves him unannounced. All of that could have been avoided if he would have just listened to us in the first place."

"Why are you always so hard on James? Have you ever been this hard on Michelle?"

"James is the oldest. He has so much unrealized potential. If he would only leave the foolishness alone."

"Why keep him as pastor of the church then?"

"I don't have any proof of anything he's done; I just know that he hasn't always been on his best behavior. He likes to test the waters. It's only a matter of time before the wave overtakes him." Edward shook his head and sighed.

All they could do was wait.

****

Grace had suspected that she was pregnant, and that's why she wanted to wait to announce their engagement. She had taken a test and it came out positive. She took another one, a few days later, and that one was positive too. She rationalized in her mind that the tests could still be wrong, so she had called her doctor and scheduled an appointment. Since she wasn't *completely* sure yet, she didn't want to bring it up and cause unnecessary worry.

If she and James had been able to just get married, without any complications, no one would figure that they had already been together for almost eight months. A pregnancy changed *everything*. How were they going to handle this?

She also had to figure out how to tell James. *Real cute Grace, getting knocked up by your pastor. Ugh! I can't take this right now.* Maybe James would be happy. She knew he wanted a family. But Grace also knew that neither of them was expecting this to happen... at least not now. Maybe they had hoped that their inconsistent to gradually non-existent use of contraception wouldn't matter. Grace emotionally considered all the different ways he could possibly react. In the end, she decided to trust that he would help her through this. He loved her... he promised he would take care of her and they were engaged, so that had to mean something. *I can trust him. He won't let me down.*

Despite her self-encouragement, Grace found herself acting withdrawn around James. She suspected it was only going to be so long before he brought it up.

Late one night, a few days later, they were settling in at Grace's apartment. Grace sensed an intense gaze aimed her way. She sighed, turned to face James and gave him a questioning glance.

"What's wrong?" he asked. "You've been withdrawn, emotional and moody for days. Did something happen?"

Grace's appointment was in two days, so she still couldn't tell him yet. "No, nothing happened. I just haven't been feeling well. I'm going to the doctor on Friday." She gave him the most briefly detailed answer she could and she hoped he would leave it alone. She laid down and closed her eyes. *Please take the hint James. Leave it alone.*

"Grace."

Grace sighed again, this one deeper, slower, longer and louder than the first one. As the months had passed, he had taken a liking to calling her Grace every now and then, but usually only when he was either irritated with her, or if he was really trying to get her attention. For some reason, it always had the same grating effect on her nerves.

Eyes still closed, she answered. "What?"

"Did I do something to you? I feel like you're shutting me out."

Grace was immediately contrite. She wasn't trying to make him feel bad. She opened her eyes and sat up.

"No James, you didn't do anything to me. I'm sorry about

my moods... I've just been a little irritable."

"Are you sure that's all? You've barely let me touch you for the past four days."

Grace reflected on his words, feeling the instant accompanying desire. Her body seemed to come alive from a four-day reprieve. That may have had something to do with her moods, too. Only once before had they gone this long without being intimate. She had been so preoccupied with worry that she shut out everything from the outside, as much as she could.

She rested her hand on his cheek. "I'm sorry. It's really not you. I don't mean to shut you out."

"You don't want to tell me right now what's going on with you, so just let me be there for you. Let me comfort you," he coaxed, kissing her with great care. He kissed her lightly and she loosened up as he guided her to go along with him.

Grace could no longer deny herself what she craved. They were both driven with a strong, almost overpowering desire, one that demanded immediate satisfaction.

Later, James was holding Grace while she slept. He marveled at their many levels of desired pleasure. Every month it seemed to intensify to a greater degree. They needed to get married soon, or else they might get careless. He studied Grace as she slept in his arms. Something was going on with her, something she wasn't telling him. She wasn't withdrawn and having mood swings for no reason. She chalked it up to not feeling well, and he decided to let her off with that explanation this time. She had become irritated with his questions, and he hadn't wanted to risk an argument with her. But they would definitely talk after her doctor's appointment.

Chapter 10

Grace sat in her apartment, curled up on her couch, in the dark. She had been crying for hours—her suspicions clearly confirmed. James had been calling her for hours too, trying to check on her, no doubt. He had come by earlier and tried to use his key, but she had the bolt locked, so he couldn't get in. She would eventually have to face him, but she couldn't do it right now.

Figuring he was probably worried about her, she sent him a text message:
Grace: I'm fine.
James: No, you're not. Call me.
Grace: Not now. I'll talk to you later.
James: Nylah... Grace... Call me.

Grace didn't message him back. He tried calling her again, but she would not answer. She couldn't remain closed off forever, though. After a few minutes she received another text message.
Dani: Gracie... r u okay?

Surely James had spoken to at least one of them.
Grace: Hey Dani. I'm just resting.

It was true; she was resting.

Dani: U didn't answer my question. What's wrong, honey?

Not responding, Grace's thoughts swirled in her head. *More than you could possibly guess. I have completely screwed up... in more ways than one.* Grace cried, knowing the worst hadn't even begun to happen.

Dani: James said I should check on u. Can I come over? He said something was wrong and u won't talk to him.

Grace: I'll let you come but don't tell him... and DON'T bring him or Lawrence with you!

Dani: Promise. There in a few...

Grace knew she should be talking to James, but right now she needed a girlfriend. She knew Dani would be extremely hurt and disappointed in her, but would not react based on those feelings.

Fifteen minutes later there was a soft knock. Grace went to the door and confirmed that it was Dani—only Dani. She turned on a light, but just enough to see around.

Dani came in and hugged Grace who made no effort to contain her tears. They made their way over to the couch and Dani sat down, pulling Grace down with her. She laid Grace's head on her lap and stroked her hair as Grace sobbed. The two friends had shed plenty of tears with each other over the years, but this was different. She had never seen Grace like this and she was alarmed.

"Honey, what's happened? What's going on?" Dani's voice was soothing to Grace's emotions, but she wasn't able to quite calm down.

"Ssshhh, it's okay. It's okay, Gracie."

That just seemed to make it worse. "No—it's—not—o-kay," Grace managed in between sobs.

"What happened?" Dani asked again.

"You're going to be so—upset—with me," Grace sobbed.

"I'm here for you, honey. I'm here. Whatever you need from me, you have it. No matter what."

Grace slowly calmed down enough to talk more

coherently. "Oh Dani, I've really messed up."

Dani could not possibly fathom what Grace could have done, but it must have been bad. "How so? Does this have to do with the trouble you alluded to at my house?"

Grace nodded and took a deep breath, but kept her head on Dani's lap. She wouldn't be able to confess and see her reaction at the same time. "I'm pregnant."

Silence. Dani had ceased stroking Grace's hair, an air of deafening disbelief swirling around her.

"What? Gracie are you sure?" Dani knew it was a stupid question the moment she uttered it. Grace would never tell her something this big if she wasn't certain.

"I tested positive twice. I went to my doctor and found out for sure today. Dani, I don't know what I'm going to do," Grace stated.

Dani resumed stroking Grace's hair. "Oh Gracie, who has done this to you?" Her question was asked more in awe—she wasn't expecting an answer. After a few silent moments passed, Dani asked more questions. These, she was hoping to get answers to. "So, what about the father? Does he know yet? Who is he? How long has this been going on?"

"No, I haven't told him yet."

"And…"

"We've been together-secretly-for a while, but Dani, I can't tell you who he is. At least not yet."

Secrets. Okaaay. "I knew something was going on with you. I felt it a few times, but I never did enough to try to help you."

Grace shook her head. "You asked. What else could you have done?"

"Is this why you didn't want to see James?"

Grace sat up to face Dani. "I couldn't do it. Not today. Please, don't tell him. I'll do it, I just needed some time."

"Gracie, you two were getting so close. What happened?"

Grace tried to think how best to explain without totally lying since Dani was entirely oblivious to Grace and James' relationship. "It's been really good with James. This person... though we spent some time together recently, and... now... this."

Dani's eyes were filled with a mixture of disappointment, love and concern. "Gracie..."

Grace bowed her head in shame. "I know, Dani. I know."

They sat in silence for a while, each not knowing what to say.

Finally, Grace spoke first. "You can tell Lawrence. But please make sure he doesn't tell James. I'll do it. It has to come from me."

Dani nodded, wiping her eyes. "Promise. And I'm here for you. I mean that." Dani was hurt, but she also knew that she was going to have to protect Grace. Things were about to get really hard for her.

"Thank you," Grace whispered. "I'm so blessed to have a friend like you."

"I love you, Gracie."

"I love you, too."

They embraced before Dani left. Grace knew she had much to consider.

****

"WHAT!" Lawrence exclaimed. "Grace is pregnant?"

Dani sat, slowly nodding her head. Lawrence had known something was wrong when he saw his wife's face, but he wasn't ready for this news.

"What is going on? What is going on?" Lawrence asked in disbelief.

"I know. I'm just as shocked, if not more so than you. Especially because this is Grace. I thought I would be able to see something like this coming..."

"How long has this been going on?"

"I don't know. When I got to her apartment, she was a mess. I spent a great deal of time just calming her down."

Lawrence sat back and sighed heavily, wondering how this news was going to affect James.

"Has she told James yet?" Lawrence asked Dani.

"No, not yet and she expressed that neither of us tell him. She said she'll do it."

Lawrence shook his head in disbelief. "Did she tell you who she's been with?"

Dani shook her head. "She said she couldn't tell me yet, so I don't really have any details. I honestly don't know how much more I can take though."

"Man, this is going to crush James. Why would she do something like this? If she was going to be with someone else, she should have just turned James down. Now he has to contend with this—after everything he went through with Janelle."

"I know… I know. I feel really bad. I would not have tried to get them together if I had even suspected she was seeing someone," Dani lamented. "What are we going to do?"

"We have to wait until Grace tells James. I know she's trying to figure everything out, but she need not drag her feet. I will not have us stuck in the middle of this. That won't help anybody, so she needs to talk to him soon."

Dani fell quiet. She was in between zones. Part of her was listening to Lawrence and the other part was trying to compartmentalize her racing thoughts.

"If our heads are spinning," Lawrence continued, "just imagine the reeling James is going to feel." He stopped and noticed Dani's mood had changed. "Babe," he said, eyeing her carefully, "what's wrong?"

After several moments, Dani met his gaze with her glossy one. "Grace is pregnant. I don't know how I'm supposed to feel."

Lawrence sat down in front of her and grabbed her hands. "About Grace, or about us?"

Dani paused again. "Both. I don't know how to deal with Grace's situation yet, but… what about you? I know we talked about it, but—"

"And we agreed that we would do it our way, in our time. Nothing's changed," Lawrence said.

"Maybe we should start trying. Or look into adoption."

Lawrence caressed Dani's face. "Give it some time. We'll know what to do in time. What I don't want is for us to make an emotional decision." Lawrence gently kissed her on the lips. "Okay?"

Dani nodded. "Okay." She was grateful for another reminder of why she both loved and respected her husband. His wisdom and patience always made her heart smile.

****

James did not understand. Grace had completely shut down on him. He suspected her appointment didn't go well, but he couldn't reach her. He had been worried sick after he couldn't get into her apartment. He thought maybe something had happened to her. The text she sent him was little relief. *Was she sick?* Maybe it had nothing to do with her appointment. Maybe she received some bad news about her family. But why wouldn't she tell him, if that were the case? No... it had to do with her. He was sure of that much.

James thought long and hard about the possibilities. She said she wasn't feeling well. Her behavior had been erratic, to say the least. If she wasn't sick then... James quickened with dawning. *Maybe she's pregnant.* Those were the only two possibilities that made sense. And he was more than willing to guess which one made more sense... which would explain a lot of the past month. Was she going to tell him? Yes, he was sure she would. He would give her a little more time. That's probably what she needed. *A baby!* Feeling the rapid tempo of his heart beating, he realized that he probably needed some time, too.

****

Sunday came around, Grace no better now than she had been on Friday. She still hadn't spoken to James, and she wasn't sure how she would react about seeing him. She was really nervous to tell him. After all they had been through, some things were still difficult. This was one of those things.

She got to church right before morning service started and sat with Dani. She met James' examining gaze long enough to convey they would speak later.

"You didn't talk to him did you?" Grace leaned over to ask Dani.

"No. He found out that I saw you, but he respected your privacy when I told him our conversation was confidential."

As the service flowed, condemnation rested heavily upon Grace. This time, she couldn't stay in her seat. She went to the altar and cried… for relief, for strength, for forgiveness. She found herself repeating, "I'm sorry," over and over again. Someone prayed for her and she stayed for a while until she was calm enough to return to her seat.

Dani squeezed Grace's hand. "You're going to be okay," she told her.

Grace wasn't so sure.

James had watched Grace at the altar, feeling a heavy thud in his gut. He felt a different level of shame. He had usually allowed himself to push away any feelings of negativity or guilt, but Grace's conscience, along with his own, had begun to work him over. He still wasn't to the point of ending their relationship, but he definitely had a few spiritually defining moments in his private time with God. He had allowed himself to get to a bad place, consequences looming all about. God was extremely displeased with him and it had more of a sobering effect than he thought possible. James sensed that everything was about to change… and he had a feeling that it may not be for the better.

The four of them went out to dinner. Grace didn't know why she had agreed to it and the longer it went on, the more she regretted it. Their conversations were filled with irritating, awkward moments of silence. Her unmentioned pregnancy was the elephant in the room. Grace didn't know if James even suspected it, but he didn't know from her, which would make him the only one out of the loop. After a while, they had all had enough.

Grace sucked it up. She had to break the ice with him, but they could not talk about it here.

"James, we need to talk," Grace stated. She promised she heard both Dani and Lawrence exhale in relief.

"We do," he nodded. "Later. Not here."

Grace nodded. Eventually, they paid for their meals, getting ready to leave.

Arm in arm, Dani and Grace sauntered outside. "Are you going to tell him?" she asked.

"Yes, I have to. I can't avoid it any more. He deserves to hear it from me."

"Do you need me? Do you want me to come by later?"

Grace smiled at her concern. "No. I can handle James. I'll be drained later anyway."

"All right, but if you change your mind, I'm there. Okay?"

"Okay. You don't know how much your support means to me. I love you."

"Oh, I love you too, honey," Dani replied, hugging Grace.

Grace went home and waited for James. He arrived about an hour later, anxious to see her… talk to her.

"Hey," he said, closing the door behind him.

"Hi," she said, slowly approaching him. They paused briefly before embracing. One kiss led to another and they were soon in bed, not able to help themselves.

James gently kneaded down her spine—Grace, wrapped in his arms. It always felt good to hold her.

"Nylah," he started.

"Hmmm?" Grace sat up slightly.

"Baby, what's going on? I'm really concerned about you."

Grace's eyes watered as she brought her gaze to meet his. *So much for staying strong.* "James, I'm pregnant."

As I suspected… James exhaled, finally relieved to know the reason behind Grace's emotional behavior. He grabbed her hand and squeezed it in his. "How far along are you?"

"About eight weeks."

Wow. James cleared his throat. "So—uhhh… you're not thinking about—"

Grace sat up fully, with a wild blaze in her eyes. "Thinking about what?" she asked with covered calmness.

"About getting an abortion, are you?" James knew the answer, but he had to hear it from her just to be sure.

Grace snatched his shirt in fury. "NO!!!" She scrambled off the bed and put it on before turning to face him. "I'm NOT thinking about getting an abortion. Are you thinking about *asking* me to get one?"

What? Whoa… she had misunderstood his reason for asking. He had to calm her down before things got out of hand. "No, baby. I would never consider the thought. That's not why I brought it up."

Grace glared at him, not sure if he was telling her the truth or just placating her for now.

James sensed her uncertainty, so he had to make sure she understood. He got out of bed, pulled on his pants and beckoned for her. He kissed her, took her hands and led her out of the room to the couch.

"Sit down, please," he requested.

She did and he sat next to her. "I only asked you that because I needed to hear from you that you want to have this baby. I don't know how you feel about all of this and I just need to know where your head is."

"Of course I want to have this baby. I know the situation is different from what we planned, but it's the situation we're faced with. What about you, James; do you *want* this baby?" Grace felt vulnerable and emotionally erratic.

"Yes Nylah, I do." He kissed her again and again. He placed his hand on top of her stomach and whispered, "Our baby. This is our child." He stretched out on top of her, showering her with love and affection.

Grace now felt more at ease—he wanted the baby, too. Maybe things wouldn't turn out so badly after all.

Chapter 11

James sat in his office, his mind laden with heaviness. Grace told him two weeks ago about the baby. He had stayed with her the rest of the week, spending that time talking about what would happen, and trying to make preliminary, logistical preparations. They were both aware that she would lose her job, since she worked at the church. Her pregnancy out of wedlock clearly went against the moral standards in the bylaws of the church and thus, when brought to the attention of the board, would result in the termination of her job. James told her he would financially take care of her and the baby, but there remained great uncertainty about the progression of their relationship. To everyone except Lawrence and Dani, their relationship would be a complete surprise. A sudden marriage and news of Grace's pregnancy would cause suspicion and scrutiny that James wanted to avoid, if possible. They concluded that they would have to put their marriage plans on indefinite hold. They both wanted to find a solution that would cause the least amount of controversy.

James met with the church board last week and he officially terminated Grace's position yesterday. He noted the irony in their situation. Grace had been at his house since last week, so after their "official conversation," he went home. She was still there and they just fell into their regular swing. She had known the termination was coming, but he had called her back in today and she was about to be completely blindsided... James was sick thinking about how the outcome of their conversation would directly affect their relationship.

Grace knocked on his office door before coming in. He stood to greet her, knowing that she would be far from smiling at him when she left.

"Hey, Nylah," he said.

"Hi, James. Or should I call you, Pastor Garrison right now?"

James shook his head, feeling the weight on his shoulders. "Please, don't. Always James."

They stood in an awkward silence for a few moments before Grace spoke.

"Is it okay for me to hug you?"

James smiled and they embraced for a while before he released her. He quietly observed her before he went back to his seat, feeling anxious.

"This feels strange. I've been summoned to the Pastor's office," she said as she sat down. "Why?"

James cleared his throat, feeling nervous. "Uhh, it's official business. As you know, your job had to be terminated because of violations against the moral standards of the church."

Grace regarded him with caution. "Yes, we went over this yesterday. Was there something you missed?"

James hesitated. *She's going to hate me for this.* "Nylah, you can't be active in ministry. I have to sit you down," he stated.

Grace closed her eyes. She had actually known this would

be next, but hearing it didn't make it easier. "I know. I'm far from surprised, actually. When?"

"Effective immediately, but publicly tomorrow... after Bible class."

Grace nodded, noting a nagging sensation that something wasn't right. She sat back and mentally went through this brief exchange, filtering what had just been said. *He said* he's *sitting* me *down. But, what about—*

Grace jerked up at the realization, noticing James diverting his glance away from her. "Am I being sat down *alone?*" she asked.

James nodded briefly, not able to meet her gaze.

"What about you? *We've* been together for months! This baby is *ours,* not just mine. Did I miss something?" Grace was becoming enraged.

James finally met her angry stare, his eyes watering. "Nylah, I'm sorry."

WHAT! Grace could not believe this. "You're SORRY! Are you serious? Was this your bright idea? Is this how you're supposed to take *care* of me?"

"Nylah, please calm down," James pleaded.

"I will NOT calm down to pacify you." Grace's tears streamed down her face. It never crossed her mind that James would pull something like this. "You're going to make me go through the most humiliating, albeit self-imposed, experience of my life *alone?* Why are you doing this to me?"

"Baby, I'm not trying to hurt you. But what else am I supposed to do right now? I'm the pastor... I have to do this."

"Don't. Don't call me anything other than my name. I can't believe you, James! You have the nerve to spit that "I'm the pastor" foolishness at me? Were you so concerned about being the pastor when you propositioned me for a relationship? Did it ever concern you those nights, those *weeks* we spent in each other's beds? All the trips, all this time we've been together, did you care about being the pastor then?"

"You never resisted. You never said no." James' voice was low and raspy, as he tried to reason with her in his own way.

Grace glared at him in disgust. "Is that the best you can do? How good of you to throw that in my face. But you can't. I know I'm fully responsible for my part in our relationship. The difference between us right now is that I'm willing to face the consequence. You are not."

"Nylah, it won't look right if I take no action."

"I DON'T CARE what it looks like, James!" Grace's voice raised a few levels. "This isn't even about you not taking action. This is about your unwillingness to stand by me and take responsibility for your own actions." Grace took pause, glowering with angry hurt. "This is not right. But I guess I shouldn't be surprised."

"Nylah, please—"

"You know, since you're so caught up in appearances, maybe you would like to know that, from where I stand, it appears that you are a coward. You're only concerned about yourself right now." Grace's heart hurt more than she thought possible. Is this the man she fell in love with?

"Look, I know it's difficult to—"

She cut him off. "Save it. There is nothing you can say to me right now that I want to hear from you."

"Please, try to understand my position. I don't know how else to handle this right now," James pleaded with her.

Grace oozed an air of contempt toward him. She spoke quietly, but her words were cutting, slicing straight through James without effort. "Well, I guess any noble man would do the honorable thing. It must take a man of a different caliber to so willingly ask for and involve himself in a mutual, sexual relationship and let his lover take the fall for him."

She was angry... she had more than every right to be. He completely messed up her life and was essentially asking her to be okay with his decision. She didn't deserve this from him. It was obvious he could gather no more words—words she didn't want to hear anyway.

"Nylah... I'm so sorry." James felt dejected, like a complete idiot.

"Of course you are. But not nearly as much as I am." With that, she grabbed her purse and started to leave.

"Wait!" James implored. "Please, don't go... not like this."

Grace let out a frustrated, anguished laugh. "How would you have me to leave, James? Happy? Glad that you've finally decided to check-in to your pastoral duties, at *my* expense? Overjoyed that you don't seem to mind everyone knowing my sins, but refuse to share yours? Pick one." Grace was dumbfounded by his need for her to understand his feelings.

He reached out to her. She stepped away, knowing she would cave under his touch.

"No. Do NOT touch me. It would be very wise for you to leave me alone."

"Please, forgive me. Can you forgive me?"

Grace shook her head, appalled at his audacity. "You ask a lot of me don't you? Don't hold your breath." Grace felt the movement of her right hand, but wasn't entirely conscious of the action. She had removed her engagement ring and set it on James' desk, not wanting to touch him. "I'll be out of your house by the time you get home." She turned for the door.

"Nylah..."

She turned back to him briefly before leaving. "You can call me Grace... like everybody else."

James stood at the door for a few moments, wondering... hoping she would come back. He was being selfish. This was transitioning into the hardest time of her life, a time that she wouldn't even be experiencing if it weren't for him. He was supposed to be able to comfort her, but he was the cause of her pain; she would not allow him to come near her now. He locked the door and slowly wandered back to his desk, sinking into his chair.

When James got home later, his house was quiet. He roamed from room to room. Every tangible trace of Grace was gone, but every room held a memory of her: her sound, her smell, her playfulness. By the time he got to his bedroom, he felt numb. He sat on the floor, leaning against her side of his bed. It wasn't until he touched his face that he realized he was crying.

****

Lawrence was wrapping up Bible class. James had asked him to carry the service and handle the announcement about Grace, who was huddled close to an exit door with Dani right beside her. Lawrence told the congregation that Grace would not be active in ministry for the length of time necessary to complete her restoration process. This would be a time for her to receive spiritual guidance to help her restore her relationship with God. A stunned hush fell over the church as Lawrence called Grace up to the front.

Grace went up to publicly apologize to the church, barely able to speak. She couldn't avoid the faces of all the youth, who were no doubt hurt, upset and disappointed in her. They admired her and she let them down. By the time she finished, many others were crying along with her, shocked and in disbelief at her predicament. Grace, herself, never thought she would ever be in this position. But she had not guarded her heart and now was paying dearly for it. She had managed to glance at James twice while she was talking, and both times he was staring at the floor. *He can't even face me. Why am I covering for him? He doesn't deserve it.* But she knew she didn't have the strength to tell all. Not out of spite. That was dirty, and not her style, regardless of what he'd done. When she got back to her seat, Dani, who had been crying, hugged Grace and held her close.

Right before the benediction, Dani leaned over to Grace. "Let's go, Gracie. Let's go now."

They rushed towards the doors, hoping to avoid the crowd.

Right after the benediction, James rushed to his office. The whole time Grace was talking, all he could hear was her anguish and the voice in the back of his head calling him out as a hypocrite, challenging his audacity. He knew he was going to be sick... he had to get out of there. Lawrence caught up to him at his car.

"Hey, man... you all right?"

James pulled his cap lower. He knew Lawrence probably thought that his mood was due to the fact that he was hurt about Grace. He had no idea.

"Uh... I just need to go. It's been a hard night."

"You really liked her, didn't you?" Lawrence asked.

"Look, it's not the time or the place to talk about it. I'll catch up to you later."

"All right. Take it easy, man."

****

At Grace's apartment, Dani sat with her for a little while, soaking up the night's events.

"Gracie... can you tell me now who the father is?"

Grace felt pained, carrying the weight of her secret. She shook her head slowly. "No, Dani. I can't tell you. I'm sorry."

Dani just examined Grace thoughtfully. After a while, she stood and paced the room.

"No, I'm sorry for asking."

"It's okay, you don't have to apologize."

"It's not like you to keep secrets, however, it's none of my business and you don't need me hounding you about it. I guess I'm just trying to figure out, in my mind, how and when all this started. And to figure out whom, on-this-earth-kind-of-man, was able to get you to this point."

"I know you're curious about a lot of things... I would be too. I can give you some story fillers; I just can't tell you everything."

Dani sat again, eager to let Grace tell her however much she felt able to share.

"Do you want a snack? We can talk over brownies," Grace offered, grabbing a tin of brownies her cousin had shipped to her from The Brownie Shop. She sat across from Dani, took a deep breath, and recognized relief to be able to finally open up about her relationship with James.

Grace picked up a turtle brownie she'd been craving and started slowly... thoughtfully. "It started around the end of January. We went out casually at first. Just as friends. He pursued me, and then we started to actually date... becoming affectionate. That affection turned into something more intense. We had a few encounters that left me blushing... to say the least." Seeing Dani's face, Grace rushed to continue. "I know, I know—I should have put a stop to it. But I didn't. I allowed myself to get to a place where I didn't want to stop it. So much so, that when he asked me to sleep with him the first time, I said yes. I cried... but I also stayed. Ever since then, we were pretty inseparable."

Dani exhaled and closed her eyes for a moment. "But how, Gracie? We never saw you with anyone." She munched into a brownie. "Mmmm," she hummed, briefly distracted. "Gracie, this is really good! Where did you get these?"

"Girl, Bre had them sent from Texas. The Brownie Shop... You can order them online. They came right on time too. Between my varying moods and emotions, these chocolate, walnut, caramel delights have done wonders for me."

"I can only imagine the cravings and mood swings you must be having." Dani paused before bringing the conversation back around to Grace's story. "Okay, but Gracie there was no one around."

You saw me with James plenty of times. Just not in a way to make you suspicious. "I know... I had to be careful. He would come over late at night, spend the night or week—"

"Week?" Dani asked, eyes like saucers.

"Week," Grace affirmed. "We would spend the week together either at my place or his. We tried to be as careful and discreet as possible."

"And the whole time, you never thought about your relationship with God?"

Grace's eyes became sad, her voice dropped to a whisper. "I thought about it all the time. I thought about how much I was letting God down, how upset he must have continuously been with me... all of it. But I never let it get me to the point of ending my relationship. Dani, you have to understand... I knew what I was doing. It was my choice. I can't blame him for what has happened..."

"Is he going to do what's right for you and the baby? What is his spiritual status? Gracie, does he love you?"

Grace thought about her conversation with James yesterday. She was pretty sure *that* wasn't love. "I don't know what's going to happen with him. We were supposed to get married, but that has been put on hold... indefinitely. Circumstances have strained us. He says he loves me, and that he wants this baby too, but his actions don't quite line up with his words. We're not on good terms right now." It pained her to verbalize the change in her relationship with James. It was very hard to deal with.

"He must be a Christian. I don't see you with a worldly person. Although, I never thought I'd see you in this position either."

"You would be surprised... More so than you are right now."

Dani shook her head. What a saga this had been. Grace had been with a man for more than half the year and she didn't know it. She had suspected something was going on a few times, but never this.

"Dani, I know you're upset and disappointed in me. I'm sorry. I'm sorry for everything."

"Look honey, you don't need my forgiveness. I just want you to get on the right track. You're going to be a mommy. So you have to get it together with God, so you can be okay."

Grace nodded, feeling emotional. "I don't deserve your

friendship. I have deceived you for months."

"We're friends. You don't have to tell me *everything*. And that doesn't make our friendship any less valid. You will always be my Gracie and I am always here for you."

"Thanks, Dani. Thank you so much." They hugged, Grace grateful that she still had one true friend.

Pulling apart, Dani asked, "So, whatever happened with James? I thought everything was going well."

The mention of James made Grace's heart flutter. She was still livid with him... and extremely hurt. But she loved him, too. Grace deliberately closed the tin of brownies, needing to move or somehow preoccupy her hands.

"Uhh, James and I had good interaction with each other. We had a good time when we hung out, but... my feelings and relationship with this other person was stronger and it pulled me back to him every time. Ummm... how is James taking this?"

"Not well. I think he was really starting to have strong feelings for you—"

Grace pretended to inspect a nearby wall.

"—and this took him by surprise. He hasn't said much, but he's really been in a mood lately. He's definitely not himself."

Grace wasn't sure how to respond, so she just said nothing. Dani stayed a little while longer but when she left, Grace tried to unwind. She felt a little high-strung from the series of events that had taken place the last few weeks. She had to take it easy if she didn't want her drama to add any stress to her pregnancy. Thinking about her baby, she placed a hand on her stomach. *I'll do whatever I have to do to keep you safe and healthy. I don't know what's going to happen with us, but just know that I love you, baby.*

"I love you, baby."

James had said that to her plenty of times. *James.* Grace shook her head, still in disbelief about his actions. She picked up her phone, contemplating whether to call him or not.

Sometimes she wanted to talk to him and sometimes she didn't, but she didn't have enough time to decide... her phone rang just then and it was him.

Taking a full, deep breath, Grace answered, "Hello."

"Hey Ny—Hi, Grace."

Grace noted the name change. After all, it was by her instruction. She just hadn't expected to feel so weepy about hearing it. *These emotions... UGH! Just keep it in check.*

"What do you want?" her tone, short.

"Can we talk? Please?"

"I don't want to talk to you."

"I know, Grace. I just... Can I just come for a little while?"

"James, if I don't want to speak to you, do you really think I want to tolerate seeing you?"

He was quiet for a few. "I'm miserable. I hate what I have done to you. I *need* you, Nylah. I need to see you. Talk to me. Please." He was begging and he didn't care. Every word was true.

Grace felt her heart soften towards him a little. *Probably a bad idea.* "What do you want from me, James?"

"I just want to come over. I won't stay long."

Grace thought for several moments. "Fine. Just for a little while," she gave in. "Use your key to come in." *A very bad idea.* "Make sure you leave it here when you go."

James paused, taking in the change. "Um, okay. Thank you. I'll be there in a few minutes."

Why did I just do that? Because you love him. Grace's heart and mind battled within. She would find out which choice was right.

James arrived in ten minutes, calling out to her. She felt the tears in her eyes as she met him halfway in the room. Stopping in front of him, they spoke no words. Grace determined that he must be struggling, just like her. *Good. Serves him right.*

She lifted a hand to his unshaven cheek and ran it along

his jaw. "You look terrible. Sleeping much?"

James exhaled deeply. "I can't sleep at all. All I keep hearing are your words, the hurt in your voice and the one in the back of my head, calling me a hypocrite."

"Well, you are a hypocrite, James. That should not be news to you. The both of us have been hypocrites for several months."

"I know. I'm so sorry for hurting you. It was torture to sit there while you were talking to the church."

Grace dropped her hand and moseyed over to the couch. "Well, at least you had the minute decency to have Lawrence handle it," she said, sitting down. "I guess I can thank you for that much. Having Dani with me helped. It feels really good to have at least one person I can depend on."

James involuntarily flinched. Their relationship had changed, seemingly overnight.

"What do you want to talk about?" Grace asked.

James sat next to her. "First, I wanted to apologize. And then tell you that I'm trying to figure out the best way for me to come clean."

Grace watched him warily. "Forgive me if I don't believe you. I'm still having a hard time processing your most recent actions, which don't happen to corroborate with your words."

"Is everything that we had, lost? This can't be the end."

His proximity to her had a strong physical effect on Grace. "I don't know what's going to happen, James. A lot has definitely changed between us in a short amount of time. But we are having a child—together. We're going to have to figure out something."

James had taken her hand in his while she was talking. He brought it to his mouth and kissed it. A shock surged through her veins, all meeting in one central location. She snatched her hand back and stood.

"I'm still angry with you. You hurt me more than I thought possible. Don't think everything is just okay because

I'm pregnant with your child."

"Do you still love me?" he asked, coming toward her.

She turned and moved away slowly, contemplating her answer.

"Do you?" he asked again.

Grace felt his presence behind her. She turned again to face him, but kept her head down. "Of course I still love you. That's not the point." Grace felt herself giving in and she didn't think she was strong enough to fight it. "You need to leave."

"Why?" he asked, inching closer to her.

Grace felt her heart beating at a louder, quicker pace. Her breathing became heavier. "Because if you don't, then—"

He lifted her chin to bring her gaze to his. "Then what?"

Grace wouldn't answer him. She didn't trust herself to speak further.

"Nylah," James whispered, lightly caressing the side of her face. He leaned in to kiss her. She pulled away slightly, but he came back to her and kissed her again. He kissed her for a long time.

Grace knew she was in immediate danger of giving in to him. If there was ever anything James could do, it was his ability to consume her with a kiss. Knowing this would inevitably lead them to her bed, she knew she had to stop him. Breaking away, Grace implored him with her eyes. "James, we're already in enough trouble. Too much trouble. Please, go home."

"I want to be with you. I want to stay with you. We'll work this out."

James sounded so sure of himself and that confidence ticked Grace off and snapped her back to reality. She briefly reevaluated yesterday and earlier this evening, coupled with what had just happened. *This is absurd.*

"Get out, James. You have not suffered through this with me. You haven't been there. *Dani* has been with me more than you have. You threw me under the bus to save your tail.

Don't come in here expecting to spend the night with me, in my bed, like nothing has happened."

"Nylah, I just—"

"No! I don't want to hear it. My emotions are all out of whack. Not only do I have to figure out how to get through this pregnancy, I have to sort through our relationship and get myself to an acceptable place with God."

"This is killing me, too. I'm doing my best to try and figure this out."

"Then figure it out on your own... at home. Go away. This is probably one of the most disrespectful things you can do to me right now. You have no regard for my feelings. I just had to apologize to the church today. And you want me to let you spend the night tonight? You are an outrageous piece of work."

Turning away dismissively, Grace hoped he understood how serious she was. She also hoped he would leave without needing more encouragement. Grace knew that was the right thing to do. She was just so inwardly frustrated about her conflicting feelings.

"Grace, I'm not trying to disrespect you—" James said.

"And yet you keep doing it," Grace replied.

James sighed. What had he been thinking? He needed to prioritize in the worst way. And he needed to start putting Grace's needs ahead of his own. He'd been selfish far too long.

"Okay. I'll go," James conceded. "Can we talk tomorrow... or soon?"

Grace glanced at him briefly. "Perhaps. I just need some time and distance from you."

"However much time you need, you have. I'll wait to hear from you."

James kissed her temple and left. Grace locked the door behind him. Her vision blurred when she spotted the key on her end table. She eventually found her bed and cried for the remainder of the night.

Chapter 12

"Hey, Grace."

Grace turned to the familiar voice, smiling. "Hi, Nathan! How are you?"

"I'm good. You have a few minutes? I'd like to talk to you."

Service had just ended, so they went to a quiet area of the church.

Nathan rubbed his hands together nervously, thinking about how to start the conversation. "Uhh... aside from the situation at hand, how are you doing?"

"I'm trying to do the best I can. I'm just taking it one day at a time." Grace reflected that she hadn't talked to James much in past weeks. Only a handful of times and those conversations were brief.

"I miss you, Grace... I miss our friendship. I noticed a distance between us, so I imagine it had something to do with your gentleman..." he said, motioning to her pregnancy.

"Yeah. Yeah, I kind of closed myself off from a lot of the

outer relationships I had. I'm sorry about that. I have missed our talks and our occasional dinners."

Nathan's eyes flickered with warmth. "You're still my friend, regardless. And I want you to know that I'm available to help you."

"Help how?" Grace smiled, alert with curiosity.

"Is this man taking care of you? Is he treating you right? There's a sadness in your eyes that leads me to believe he's not on the up and up."

"You've been paying close attention to me, haven't you?"

"When you had to get up in front of the church, I was really shocked. But then it made sense about you pulling away. We were great friends, and then nothing. I'd like to get back to that, at least a little."

"You mentioned help. Help me how?"

"I've given this considerable thought and I've realized that I want to take care of you. I'll take care of you and your baby."

Shock coursed through Grace's body. "Why would you want to take on that responsibility? Especially since we haven't talked for months. And the baby—the baby's not—"

Nathan stopped her. "We may have had some distance between us recently, but that doesn't take away from all the time we've had before. I can be there for you. Besides, your child doesn't have to be mine biologically, for me to want to take care of the both of you… for me to love the both of you."

Grace was incredibly fond of Nathan—as a friend. What he was offering her was as sweet as it was surprising. "You're not in love with me, Nathan. And I'm sure you're aware of the fact that I'm not really in a good place right now."

"I know. And you're right. But I still love you as a friend and I want the best for you. Or, at least the best I can offer." He flashed her his goatee-framed smile.

Grace stared into his eyes… sincere eyes. The eyes of a friend who was offering to stand by her no matter what.

How could he be so selfless? She swallowed back the emotion creeping into her throat. "What if you meet someone else?" she asked quietly. "What happens then?" Grace swallowed again. "I can't be the reason you decide to neglect your own happiness."

"If you accept my offer, then that's that. There will be no one else. My loyalty and dedication would forever lie with you and the baby. You and I will get married and be a family—and we can be happy."

Grace was extremely humbled to hear Nathan's words. It was enticing; having someone who would be dedicated to her and the baby. But what kind of relationship would they have? He didn't love her the way she needed. She didn't love him the way he deserved. *James will blow his top. I don't care what James thinks right now. Stop it!*

"Nathan, I—"

"Look, before you say no, just think about it. I won't push; I just want you to know I'm here for you and the offer stands until you decide. All right? Promise me you'll think about it?"

Grace hesitated. "All right, I promise."

Nathan took her hand and held it for a few moments. His hold felt reassuring and comfortable... but it did not illicit the same excitement Grace knew she would have gotten if James had done the same thing.

"You're a good man, Nathan. Thank you for being my friend."

Nathan grinned a charming grin. "You're welcome. Hungry?"

Grace nodded. "Famished."

"Come on. Let's go get some dinner."

As they stood to leave, Grace happened to glance up to the front of the church. She saw James staring at them, harboring a jealous glare. Grace smirked at him, trying to ignore the part of her that couldn't decide between shunning and craving interaction with him. *You think you're upset now?*

Just wait until I fill you in. Save the jealousy, James. You have no right... Shaking her head at him, she turned and left with Nathan.

Later that night, Grace heard a hard knock at her door. *I wonder who this could be,* she thought sarcastically. She had expected James to be upset, but she was a bit surprised to open the door and see him disheveled.

"What do you want?" Grace asked with as much nonchalance as she could muster.

He spit out his question. "What were you and Nathan talking about?"

"None of your business."

"I'm only going to ask you one more time. What were you and Nathan talking about?"

Grace raised her brow at his tone, demeanor and self-righteous indignation. *Oh, he can take that and leave.*

"Don't think for a moment longer," she began calmly, "that you're going to come into my house and start demanding information from a private conversation. I don't have to tell you anything."

James backed down a little, but he was still upset. "I don't like you talking to him. Are you doing this to spite me?"

"That would imply vindictiveness on my part and you aren't that important. Nathan is my friend, like it or not. And I'll talk to him whenever I want."

James could have spit nails when he saw them talking earlier and he wanted to go on a rampage when they left together. He'd realized he needed to calm down before talking to Grace. *This* was not how their conversation was supposed to go.

"You have to be the most self-serving man I have ever known," she continued. "How dare you? Like you have the right to be upset with me about anything! What is wrong with you?"

"Grace, I'm sorry. Please... I'm sorry."

"We've already established how sorry you are," Grace said

coolly.

James sat, studying Grace for a few minutes, his eyes glistening. "Your conversation with him was about something serious."

Grace regarded him for a moment. Honestly, it was at least partially his business, since it had to do with the baby. "Yes. Maybe some of it is your business," Grace relented. She crossed to the other side of the room and turned to face James. *Oh, my goodness. He is going to be livid. Should I care? Do I care? I don't know...*

"Nathan offered to take care of me... and the baby."

"Take care of you, how?" James asked carefully, sitting straight up. *Show restraint. Don't lose it.*

"He wants to marry me and be dedicated to us. He seems to observe that my former partner may not be handling his business and he has offered to fill that void."

James clenched his jaw and stood slowly. He crossed the room to Grace and stood directly in front of her. He spoke low and forceful with undeniable authority.

"No other man, especially Nathan, is going to raise my child."

"Well, if you choose not to raise him, then you have no say over who does."

"I have never said I wasn't going to raise him. We are not in a stellar situation, Grace. But we can work it out."

"What makes you think that I want to work it out, James? Huh?" Grace began to cry... again. "What have you shown me that would make me want to work anything out with you?"

James stepped back, needing to catch his breath. "You're—you're not thinking of accepting his proposal, are you?"

Grace could hear the hurt in his voice. It was almost too much for her.

"James, I—it's something for me to think about. He's offering what I need—support —stability. I need a partner that can be with me in public. I can't hide anymore. If Nathan wants to be there, maybe I should let him."

James shook his head. "No. NO! You can't. You don't love him," James said desperately. "I know we have some things to figure out, but please don't accept his offer. Just give me a little time. I'll step up. I promise."

"I don't want your words. Don't promise me something you're not able to give me."

"Nylah—"

"Why should I trust you?" Grace sighed and leaned against the windowsill. This was making her tired.

James took her face in his hands. "I love you—and our baby."

"Is this all about your pride? I don't have time to manage your ego."

"No, it's not. This is about us and our baby. I'm not going to stand by and watch you set up house with this—" He placed both hands in his pockets, but remained close to her. "I just want you to know that I'll fight for you. I will."

Grace sighed heavily. Would James really do what was necessary? Grace thoughtfully considered her response. "Listen, I have a sonogram appointment in three weeks. If you're ready to be there for us, you can start by coming to the appointment."

"Okay. Okay. I'll be there." James breathed a sigh of relief. He bent down to give her a light, grateful kiss. The effect however, was not light.

"And what about Nathan's proposal?" he asked her.

"We'll see what happens."

He kissed her lightly again.

"Are you sure, James? Because—"

"Sssshhhh," he said, pulling her up against him. "I said I'll be there. Okay?"

Grace just nodded, her mind becoming numb. She hadn't been this close to James in weeks and she was feeling dizzy.

"Uhhh, ummm, maybe you should you know, uhhh, go—

like go." *Why am I rambling like this? Get it together, girl.*

"I will. Just not yet." He gently lifted her chin and kissed her a third time with a needy intensity.

It had felt like forever since the last time they'd kissed. Grace knew she needed to pull away, but the strength of his arms around her invoked many pleasurable memories and their mutual desire burned fiercely. Grace wrapped her arms around his neck, drawing him as close as possible. She felt all of her resolve dissolving, knowing she lost all her willpower to fight him. She knew it was wrong, but she couldn't seem to help herself. She gave in to him once again.

Chapter 13

Lena saw Michelle enter the center. She was working on a coloring activity with Jade, a little girl who attached herself to Lena when she started coming to the center. Lena motioned to Michelle to meet her in her office while she finished with Jade. After a few more minutes, Lena came into her office and hugged Michelle.

"Hey!" Lena greeted.

"How is your day going?" Michelle asked. They sat on the couch in Lena's modern, classically-decorated office. Her four walls were alternately painted black and white. She sat in a purple chair at a purple-trimmed, custom black oak desk. A sizable bookcase was occupying space against one wall, filled to capacity with books. The couch, a television, a coffee table and a refreshment bar completed her office.

"Good. Our lunch wasn't for today was it?" Lena frowned. She was usually on point with remembering her appointments.

"Oh no, not at all. I just came by to see you."

"No, you didn't." Lena eyed her friend. "You never just come by and the girls aren't here today. What's going on?"

Michelle smiled. They knew each other so well. "Have you called Devin back?"

Lena sighed. "No, I haven't. I'm not interested in him."

"Have you given him a chance? He's really nice." Michelle pushed.

"No, thank you. I just don't feel it. I know he's nice and he's been a real gentleman, but he's not for me."

"You don't like anybody. Will you ever give anyone an actual shot at being with you?"

Lena shrugged. "Maybe one day. But I don't need your help, thank you."

"I know you don't need my help, I just want you to get your Boaz."

"I'm too busy to date. Besides, Boaz is dead."

"Okay. But if I notice someone for you—Wait. *What?*"

Lena chuckled. "I said, 'Boaz is dead.'"

"Girl, what are you talking about?"

Lena showed Michelle her tablet. "It's a new book I'm reading, by Mark Moore, Jr. It's really interesting. *Boaz is Dead… And 9 Other Essential Truths Every Christian Single Should Know.* And I know a few other people who need to read it."

Michelle laughed. "Careful. Everybody's not ready to receive it."

"Honey, if I don't already know! Listen, have you talked to James?" Lena asked.

Michelle's eyes clouded briefly. "Why? He's not trying to hit on you, is he?"

"Would you calm down? No. I haven't heard from him in a while."

Michelle relaxed. "No, I haven't heard from him either, which would normally concern me. But I figure maybe no news is good news. He can be so unpredictable sometimes."

"Yeah," Lena murmured.

"Why does this matter to you?" Michelle asked curiously.

Lena shrugged. "I don't know. He just crossed my mind."

"Well, don't worry about him. Trust me, if there was any reason to be concerned, we would know. Dad usually sniffs out stuff like this."

Lena wasn't sure what it was or why, but something kept nagging her about James. Once her conversation with Michelle was over, and after Michelle was definitely gone, Lena picked up her phone.

****

James was home contemplating Grace's sonogram appointment when his phone rang. "This is James."

"James, Lena."

James' brow wrinkled in surprise. "Lena! Hey. Are you okay? You almost never call me out of the blue."

"I'm all right. You crossed my mind and I just asked Michelle about you. How are you?"

James paused and sighed. "I'm not the best."

"I didn't think so. You want to talk about it?"

"I don't want to put you in an awkward position," James said, exhaling.

"I know how to keep a secret."

"I shouldn't say anything…" he said faintly.

"James… is it really bad?"

"You have to promise you won't tell anyone. It'll come out eventually, but until then, you can't say a word to anyone. Especially Michelle or my parents. And when they find out, I'll make sure they don't know that you already knew."

"Wow. It must be heavy. Well, you have my word."

Lena allowed James the few minutes he obviously needed to get himself together.

"My girlfriend is pregnant."

Lena was stunned. She knew James could be bad, but she would have given him more credit than this.

"Lena are you still there?"

"James… are you serious?"

"Completely."

"Are you still the pastor? What's going on? And who else knows?"

"I am currently still the pastor. No one else knows except me, her and now you. And I'm not telling her that I told you."

"Oh, my G—"

"I know. Lena, this is the worst situation I have ever been in."

"What are you going to do?"

"I don't know—I don't know. Everything has changed. And lately, she's been between very upset and extremely cautious with me."

"Why?" Lena demanded.

James spilled a short version of what had recently transpired between him and Grace.

"Can I just call you an idiot and be done with that part?"

"I am more than an idiot."

"Do you even love her, or were you going to marry her because of the baby?"

"Yes, I love her, but of course my actions don't exactly prove that."

Lena paused at length. Finally, she said, "I'm coming to see you."

"Why?" James said.

"Because we need to finish this conversation in person. And you need to know that, no matter what, you still have a friend. Don't worry. Michelle will not find out that I have been to see you. That's a Pandora's box I have no desire to open."

"It would be good to see you," James admitted.

"Good. I'll be there in a few days. Make sure you answer your phone."

"Got it. And, Lena... thanks."

"You're welcome."

****

Grace sat in her car, trying to get herself together. She had been crying since she left her doctor's appointment. *I am such a fool. To think I actually believed he was coming.* Grace took a few deep breaths, shaking her thoughts away.

Ever since that Sunday night when James had come over, they had been making slow progress. He had spent the night in her bed, but Grace didn't want that to become the reason they were talking on a more regular basis. She put a few necessary boundaries in place, not allowing him to be close to her when they were alone. To which, they were only alone if she went to see him at the church, or if they met at a neutral, public location.

In the few days leading up to her appointment, she could sense his nervousness. She even figured he may actually back out, but every time she asked him if he was still coming, he always said yes. When he hadn't shown to pick her up, she left on her own. She called him repeatedly and left him a few messages. *He didn't even have the decency to call and tell me he wasn't coming.* Grace could not believe he'd stood her up. When her phone rang, she rushed to pick it up but it was Dani.

"Hello?"

"Hey, Gracie! How'd your appointment go?"

"Oh, it went okay." Grace was trying to keep herself from crying in Dani's ear.

"Did he come? Was he there with you?"

Dani had wanted to go with Grace, but Grace had asked her if she would take a rain check. After a few persistent 'whys', Grace told Dani the father was supposed to come with her.

"Uhh, no honey... he didn't come." Grace felt the tears trickle down.

"I'm so sorry, Gracie."

"Yeah," Grace sighed. "Me, too."

Dani continued to try and cheer her up as she made her way upstairs to her apartment. She came to a stop... James was sitting in front of her door. He appeared distraught and had been crying. *He has some nerve.* Shaking her head at him, Grace finished her phone conversation. "Hey Dani, um, I need to go. I need to clean up some trash that's sitting in front of my door," she stated, glaring at James. "Yeah, I'll call you later. Bye."

Grace fought with most of the things she wanted to say. She felt a deep-seated, steady stream of unholy words to say to him, none of which were very lady-like. She needed to keep it clean. No doubt, she would not spare his feelings, considering that he didn't mind lately about sparing hers.

"Why would you even come here? I don't want to see you."

"Nylah. Grace. Please, let me explain."

"Explain what?" Grace snapped. "What a lousy excuse of a job you've done stepping up? Or would it be that you lack the common courtesy to call me and tell me you lied about coming? Maybe it would be that you're here now, to apologize… again, and hope that I'll let you spend the night."

James observed her: her eyes were red from crying, but cold as ice. Her voice was extremely restrained and her body was tense. He feared she wouldn't be able to forgive his most recent in a long list of transgressions against her.

"I just want to—"

"Say that you're sorry. Of course you are. Move out of my way."

"Can we talk? Can I come in?"

Grace gave him a look of disgust. She stepped inside and waited for him to come in. *Better to handle it privately, at least.*

"I should have called you. It was inconsiderate of me to not tell you I wouldn't be there."

"Inconsiderate? Okay, let's try this. Did you have an emergency, personal or otherwise?"

"No."

"Was there a circumstance beyond your control, which prevented you from coming?"

James' eyes watered. "No."

"Did you forget or lose track of time?"

James swallowed hard. "No."

"Did you leave your phone somewhere and were unable to call me?" Grace's voice was getting lighter and filled with more hurt.

"No."

She nodded, recognizing her worst fears. "Did you ignore my phone calls?"

James hesitated, trying to prolong the inevitable.

"Did you?" she asked again.

"Yes."

"Why? I asked you many times if you were coming. How come you didn't tell me? Why didn't you say something?" Grace broke down, feeling her heart breaking.

"I was coming. I was. But then a thought came to me about what if someone saw me? Then more thoughts came: they would jump to the wrong conclusion, then word would spread, and that's not how I want everything to come out. So, when I sat down and thought about everything, I felt the pressure of it all and—and I couldn't do it. I'm sorry."

"You're always sorry. You promised me, James! I told you not to say it if you couldn't give that to me, but you still promised. Yet, there I was… alone again because of you. And, wait a minute… just what exactly is the wrong conclusion that someone would come to, James? That you're the father of my baby? Why on earth would ANYbody think that?"

"I just need more time."

Grace had had and heard enough. "Fine. That is perfectly fine with me. You can take all the time you need. We're done. Don't call me; don't come to see me, nothing."

"No. Please, don't do that. I just need—"

"I just need you to leave us alone. Completely. I don't want anything from you. We don't need you. Not your money, not your presence, not your—"

"That's unreasonable, Grace. You're not working. What

will you do for money?"

"I'll figure something out. I can definitely work somewhere."

"I don't want you working right now—"

"IT'S NOT UP TO YOU what I do. My life is no longer your concern. You can go now."

James despondently turned to go, but he stopped at the door.

"Just let me send you money, to take care of everything you need. It's the least I can do for you and the baby. It'll be one less worry for you."

Grace saw in his eyes his regret at having hurt her. Not needing to be emotionally swayed, she folded her arms across her body, but remained reticent.

"I know it doesn't seem like it. I know I haven't been acting like it. But I do love you."

Shaking her head, Grace tore her gaze from his, trying to blink away her tears.

James was extremely conflicted... about everything. "Grace... Nylah. I'm sorry I keep hurting you. One day I'll find a way to stop."

Grace wiped her eyes. "I'll keep you informed about the baby. Other than that, I don't want to see you outside of church; I don't want to have any contact with you... at least for now. I need to get my head on straight and I can't do it with you."

James nodded, acknowledging that he could not fight with her. He had to let her go.

****

For days, Lena's mind wandered in her thoughts about James. He was in a terrible situation that was only going to get worse. After she had dinner, she decided to call him. "Hey James, it's me."

"Lena... hey."

"You sound worse than before. What happened?"

James gave Lena the rundown about Grace cutting him

off and why.

"Well, James," Lena started softly, "what did you expect? She's hurting right now and you are directly related to everything that's going wrong for her."

"I know," James answered despondently.

"Have you told the church yet?" Lena asked.

"No. No one else knows, still. Not even Lawrence."

"Are you just waiting for that axe to fall? It's going to come down whether you want it to or not. It would be much better if you owned up to your stuff. Otherwise, you're really going to be in for a time."

James sighed. "Yeah. I guess that pretty much sums it up. Just… pray for me Lena. I really need it."

"I will. You can count on that."

Chapter 14

Weeks later, Grace approached the church building on a Sunday morning. A few people greeted her, some smiled. People had loosened up around her a little and realize that she was the same person they had always known. A few still treated her like she had the plague, but Grace understood having to take the good with the bad. She did miss one of her friends—or former, rather—in particular. Lisa had been a good friend allowing Grace to spend time with her teenage daughter, Emma. After Grace had been sat down, Lisa completely turned her back on Grace and refused to let Emma have any contact with her. Aside from dealing with James, that was one of the hardest ordeals she had to go through.

Grace ventured toward the church office, hoping to find Dani. Her journey was interrupted.

"Excuse me, Sister Grace! May I have a word with you?"

Why? Grace rolled her eyes and turned around. Sister Valencia Reynolds stood there, waiting to be obliged. *Let's not be rude. She may actually need something this time.*

Every run-in Grace ever had with Valencia had been unfortunate. She wasn't expecting a pleasant conversation. Grace couldn't deny that part of her was feeling protective... and possessive over James. Valencia continually tried to dig her hooks into him, much to Grace's annoyance. Even though she had not spoken to James in weeks... since she told him she was cutting him out—she still loved him and would not suffer through any of Valencia's vain babblings.

Grace plastered a smile on her face. *Don't overdo it, Grace. Be nice, not fake.* "Sister Reynolds, what may I do for you?"

"I was hoping we could talk in a more private area."

Absolutely not. "I was on my way somewhere. We can talk here."

"If you insist." When Grace did not object she continued. "I am aware of your unfortunate condition."

Here we go. "I'm pregnant, Valencia. It's a baby, not an unfortunate condition. And the whole church is aware of it. Point?"

"Well, perhaps you should keep a low profile. You know, not flaunt around in front of other men, that type of thing."

Was she serious? Lord, these people... "Valencia, what are you talking about? And why are you talking about it? You have no need to discuss me or my pregnancy, much less my interactions with others."

While they were talking, Dani noticed Grace's body language and then saw who she was talking to. "Uh-oh..."

Lawrence and James joined her. "Uh-oh what?" Lawrence asked her.

"Out there." Dani pointed.

James had to catch his breath. To him, Grace exuded radiance. She had on a navy blue dress that had a lace fitted top with a full skirt, hitting just below her knee. It was the perfect fit to conceal the changes with her body. Her red pumps provided a flair he'd grown accustomed to, and her hair was curled in loose waves... the way he liked it. *And she is carrying my child...* As he watched them, James had a feeling Valencia was instigating a situation with Grace. *What in the world could they be talking about?*

The three of them observed the motions of an unpleasant exchange going on between the ladies.

"No need to be snippy," Valencia stated before smugly adding, "I'm just trying to help you."

"Hardly. Do you want something? I must be going."

"It would be wise for you to stay away from Pastor Garrison. I'm also aware that the both of you spent some time together before your... situation." Valencia motioned to Grace, casting an eye over her. "Since the both of you are close to some of the same people, I know you're around him often. He's off limits, so don't try to entice him with your wiles."

Grace shook her head. *This lady is a can of preposterous nuts. She doesn't even know what she's talking about.* "So, do you speak for James now?" Seeing Valencia's eyes grow round, Grace added, "Yes, Valencia, I call him James. You see, he and I have an actual friendship." *And a baby on the way.* "We can solve all of this by simply asking him his thoughts on whatever you think you know. But trust me, you have no idea."

"There's no need to involve him in your mess," Valencia complacently suggested. "Listen Grace, he needs a good woman—"

"And that would be you? Has James even acknowledged an interest in you?" Grace slyly asked, tilting her head to the side.

Valencia avoided answering the question directly. "He and I have gone out a few times—"

Grace recoiled. She didn't know James had gone out with her. It was technically none of her business, but... the mixture of anger, disappointment and hurt swirled around in her. The enemy lines had officially been drawn and Grace was ready to pounce. James was *her* man...or at least he had been. Either way, Valencia could *not* have him. That was out of the question. Grace turned to the office and saw Dani, Lawrence, and James watching them. She shot a steely glare James' way.

"—and there may be something there," Valencia continued. "But if you try to interfere, then he may get distracted with the possibility of other benefits. He is only a man, after all."

Grace scoffed at Valencia's audacity. "For the record, I don't need to define my relationship with anyone to you. Any interaction I have with James is none of your business, so you'd do well to stay out of it."

Valencia stepped closer to Grace, her voice low. "I mean it, Grace. Stay away. Take care of you and your—baby," she finished haughtily.

"Valencia, I've already been sat down. Don't give me cause to extend my stay."

"Am I to understand that you're threatening me?"

You're about to understand something all right. "Why would I do something like that? Just understand that James will always take my side over yours. And if he knew you were talking to me like this, he would very quickly put you in your place," Grace finished.

Valencia smirked. "I wouldn't count on it, if I were you."

James knew Valencia was trying to stir up trouble, judging by the way Grace's face was set. *I need to stop this before anything else happens.* "Excuse me," he said to Dani and Lawrence. "I'll go break them up before a brewing catfight ensues."

Grace took a breath. She knew Valencia was trying to push her buttons. *Just don't swing. She's crazy—don't let her drive you to join her.* "Valencia, the time will come when you will rue this day."

James reached them right as Grace was finishing her statement. He cleared his throat. "What's going on, ladies?"

Valencia was about to toss another snide comment at Grace, but instead she put on her most flirtatious voice and smiled. "Oh, Pastor Garrison, nothing to concern you. We were just catching up."

"No, we weren't," Grace corrected.

Valencia narrowed her eyes at Grace in what she tried to convey as a silent warning.

Grace raised her eyebrow and gave a half-smile. *Do you really think you're getting off that easy? You should not have underestimated me or my relationship with James.*

"Valencia seems to think that I am enticing you with my 'wiles', as she put it. She staked her claim and said you were off limits. Since the both of you have gone out a few times," Grace put extra emphasis on that statement, hoping it's meaning would not escape James, "she then warned me to stay away from you and to take care of me and my baby."

"And what did you say to her?" James asked cautiously.

"Why don't you ask Valencia? I gave her side, she can give you mine."

They both turned to her.

Valencia faltered, caught off guard by her unexpected contribution to the conversation. Recalling Grace's comments, she wasn't sure how much she wanted to say. "She calls you James, Pastor Garrison."

"I know that. We've been friends for years. Is that a problem for you?" James asked, in a tone that said he didn't care about her answer.

"No—well, we've been out but I still call you—" Valencia's voice feebly trailed off, too embarrassed to finish her verbalization.

"Is Grace telling the truth? Did you say all of these things to her?"

Valencia nodded.

"Why?" James asked, sternly observing her.

Valencia could sense his irritation with her. If she hoped to salvage any hope of a possible relationship with him, she had to find a way to smooth out that irritation.

"Well, I just thought she needed to—"

"This is not the way we are supposed to deal with one another—showing the biblical love that we're supposed to have for our brothers and sisters."

"She needs to stay out of my business," Grace chimed in.

James gave her a short glance. "I'll handle it, Grace." He turned back to Valencia. "I hope that if you cannot be congenial, you can at least refrain from being messy. I'm sorry, but we only went out because you offered. We do not have an established relationship outside of church."

Grace nearly choked on a laugh behind James. *She asked him out? The nerve of her coming at me like that.* Grace thought, shaking her head. It was also a relief to know it hadn't been his idea.

"You should apologize to Grace," James said.

Valencia's eyes grew wide again. Putting on her best face, she turned to Grace. "I apologize Sis. Grace, if I have offended you." Valencia then turned to James. "I apologize to you as well, Pastor Garrison. I overstepped my boundaries and it won't happen again."

Grace caught Valencia's eye and mouthed, *I told you.* Grace knew it was childish, but she couldn't resist. She gave her a cunning smile while James finished talking to her.

After Valencia left, James turned to face Grace. He inhaled her scent; he hadn't been this close to her in weeks.

"Thank you," Grace said softly, "for defending me." She started to leave but James subtly stopped her.

"My office," he said.

"Please, don't try to pull rank on me," Grace whispered.

"My office now, please."

Grace followed him to his office, feeling as if she had no other recourse.

He shut and locked the door before turning to her. "What was that all about?" James asked.

Grace threw him a darted glare. "It seems your girlfriend has a problem with me and our apparent closeness. Keep her away from me."

"She's not my girlfriend. There's only one woman able to fill that space."

Grace eyed him as he made his way to stand in front of her. "Just because you know I won't publicly defy your position, doesn't mean you can take advantage of the situation. "

"That was the only way I could get you back here to talk to you."

"Don't do it again," Grace warned.

"Duly noted. How are you?" James subconsciously grabbed her hand and held it in his. Neither of them really noticed, or they did and didn't mind for the time being.

"My doctor visits are going well, and I'm trying to be as fine as possible. It's not easy. My days are emotionally tumultuous, at best."

James was silent for a few moments. "So, uhh," he started, clearing his throat, "you've been spending time with Nathan." It was more statement than question. Nathan still remained to be a sensitive subject for them.

"I have." Grace answered lightly, "Have you been keeping tabs on me?"

"No—no, Dani mentioned it to Lawrence in my presence. Did you accept his offer?" His question sounded stiff. It was... there were two possible answers, one of which he didn't want to hear. But he had to know.

Grace sighed. "No, James. I did not... at least not yet. I can't bring myself to do it."

"Why not?" James asked, hopeful.

Grace studied him as he stood in front of her, becoming acutely aware that he was stroking her fingers ever so lightly. She didn't want to get into this kind of conversation with him. Definitely not here. She pulled her hand back and went to sit. "You went out with Valencia?" Grace's question was laced with sarcasm.

James's eyes riveted away briefly. "Yes. I'm sorry you had to hear it the way you did. But there is nothing going on between her and me."

Grace repressed an unkind retort. Instead, she shrugged it off. "It's not as if we're together. You don't owe me an explanation."

"Yes, I do. If I'm in love with you, I don't have any business going out with another woman."

Grace stared at the wall. "I know she asked you," Grace said, turning to him. "But why would you agree to it? You don't even like her. It sends the wrong message."

James leaned back against his desk and folded his arms. "The same could be said about you and Nathan."

"Don't start that, James."

"You started it. If I go out with Valencia, it sends the wrong message. But if you go out with Nathan, it's okay?"

"Nathan and I are friends. You and Valencia are not."

"Nathan asked you to marry him, and offered to take care of you and our child. No matter what he says, that's not just friendship. And the more time you spend with him, the more he may think you're going to accept his offer. Does that not send the wrong message as well?"

Grace was reflective. She had hoped that Nathan was not in love with her. He had never declared affection for her outside of friendship, but his interactions with her suggested otherwise. She had been trying to force herself to not think about it, but she wouldn't be able to avoid it forever. She also didn't want to further encourage any type of hope he had for a union between the two of them.

"Point taken," Grace agreed. "I'll handle Nathan."

"Good. You should have—" James refrained from finishing his statement, seeing the warning on Grace's face.

"I should go now," Grace said, preparing to leave.

"Can I come over later? Maybe we can finish talking."

"No. We're finished. This conversation doesn't put us back on regular speaking terms. The distance between us has been necessary and it will remain. If anything happens that you should know about, I'll inform you. Other than that…"

Grace trailed off the rest of her statement.

James nodded to her, disappointed that she still didn't want to see or talk to him, though he had come to understand and agree with her reasoning. Before turning the handle to let her out, he stopped and said, "Thank you. It was good spending some time with you."

Grace peered up at him through her lashes. James instantly recalled the first time she had done that and smiled at the memory... and at her now, in the present. Maybe it was out of habit, but she placed her hand on his chest before she whispered, "You're welcome."

He cautiously bent down and gently kissed her cheek, but touched her nowhere else. "I love you," he whispered in her ear.

Grace leaned into him slightly and closed her eyes, trying to keep the threat of tears away. "I know. Goodbye, James." Though she had not verbally returned the sentiment, he saw the truth in her eyes before she left. At least he could hold onto that for a while.

Chapter 15

Dani and Grace moved around each other in Dani's kitchen, finishing Thanksgiving dinner preparations. Grace was trying her hardest not to sample a sweet potato pie, while getting the other desserts situated. Dani pulled the macaroni and cheese from the oven, and set it next to the greens and fried turkey. Everything else was almost done.

Mmmmm... Thanksgiving! This was really the most wonderful time of the year for Grace.

"What are you thinking about?" Dani asked.

"Just about how much I love Thanksgiving!!!" Grace beamed.

Dani was glad her friend had a reason to smile. She knew Grace had been having a difficult time—both emotionally and spiritually, but she seemed to be making progress. Maybe it had to do with the separation between her and the baby's father.

Dani thought the physical changes in Grace magnified how adorable she already was. Her cheeks and her figure were fuller. Grace had always been one to be stylish while concealing her shape. It was becoming harder for her to conceal her figure, so Dani saw Grace embracing that change. They had a great time shopping for maternity clothes that met Grace's approval. For her part, Dani had come to terms with her feelings about Grace's pregnancy. With God's help, and Lawrence's support, she had been able to reconcile her emotions. After several conversations about expanding their family, she and Lawrence were now exploring their options through adoption.

"Gracie, I'm glad you came. I wasn't sure if you would, but even if you had tried to fight me on it, I was NOT about to let you stay home by yourself."

"I know. And, thank you. Your support has been paramount. I could not have gotten through many of these recent days without you."

They alternated between cooking and talking, watching the football games on TV and shooing Lawrence away when he tried to taste the food.

"Gracie."

Grace noticed Dani seemed a little pensive.

"James is joining us for dinner. His parents are in town for the holidays; they're coming with him."

Grace gulped. She had only spoken with James once since their conversation at the church. Grace had gone to James' house after one of her appointments to give him an update on the baby and some sonogram pictures; he invited her to stay and he made her a nice lunch. Grace had expected and hoped to leave with no damage done. They had started with a pleasant enough interaction, which took a more tense turn at the mention of Nathan. James said something a little more than suggestively scornful, and Grace immediately knee-jerked with a scathing reply that alluded to his absence in her life and lack of responsibility for his actions.

"I was going to call you yesterday, but I wasn't sure if you were busy, or would even talk to me," James said.

"I guess we'll never know, huh? I didn't do much. I took care of a few things and met Nathan at the park for a wal—" Grace stopped, realizing her mistake. She had not intended to mention Nathan, at the risk of firing up James. Too late.

"Nathan? He's still chasing after you?" James asked with bright blazing eyes. "You said you were going to handle him. Is he that hard up for your attention that he follows you wherever you go? He doesn't have anything better to do?"

Grace had intended to remain calm, but she took offense at James' words, especially considering that this whole mess started with him.

"Don't be mad at Nathan because he is willing to do something you're not," Grace shot back.

"What does that mean?" James angrily asked.

"Do you want to go there with me right now?" Grace replied, matching his heightened anger.

"Maybe we should just address the fact that you said you wouldn't leave me for another man," James reminded her.

"That I wouldn't leave you!" Grace responded incredulously. She threw her napkin on the table and got up. Glaring at James with tears in her eyes, she cried, "I'm not the one who left! You abandoned me James! Now, I just have to do what is necessary for me and our baby because you refuse to do what is necessary or right for all of us."

James stood from the table. "Why would you want some man who obviously can't find anybody else to be with? Is there something wrong with him?"

"Shut up, James! This is not about Nathan. This is about you and your failure to man up. Don't you dare talk to me about someone else when your issues are far from resolved."

Before its end, the conversation had turned into a nasty and ugly fight.

They both said things they shouldn't have.

James approached Grace but stopped, leaving some distance between them. "If you accept Nathan's offer, the both of you will live to regret it. I promise you that."

Grace bore her gaze into him, not intimidated by his words. "You know what James, I wish you would. I WISH you would!" Moving around to gather her things, she kept talking. "You stand in no position to make such 'promises.' I will make sure that everybody we know fully understands the nature of our relationship and that you are this baby's father." With all of her things in hand, she turned to face him one final time, angry tears streaming down her face. "And then I will cease all contact with you, move away if need be, and you will never be a part of this child's life. Try me if you want to. But don't say I didn't warn you."

The both of them were seriously smarting when she left.

Grace had been upset with him. So much so that it showed in some of her interactions with other people. Her attitude had probably led Dani to believe she wouldn't come to dinner. Thankfully, Dani was not one to allow Grace to wallow in self-pity.

"Are you okay with him being here? I know you two haven't been on the best of terms lately."

"It's okay. I'm the one that hurt him," Grace choked out. "Does he know I'm coming?"

Dani nodded. "Lawrence told him. He seemed fine with it."

Of course he did. Grace didn't know how he would feel about seeing her… she was trying to figure out how she felt about seeing him. She could scarcely believe it had been nine months since they went out for their first date. Seemed like a lifetime ago.

She and Dani continued talking while they were finishing up the details: dinner was ready, table was set, and the Cowboys were playing. The doorbell rang and Grace heard Lawrence greet James. She heard James' mother's voice giving a cheery appreciation for the dinner invitation. Dani mentioned to Grace something about not wanting to be a rude hostess before she joined them and greeted her houseguests. Grace stayed put in the kitchen.

Grace had met James' parents several times before. She and James' mother had been able to cultivate a wonderful relationship over the years. She even got along with his father, though she had not spent as much time around him. She knew that James' relationship with his father was strained, but that remained one of their least discussed subjects.

Dani came back to the kitchen with James' parents and Grace happily greeted them. While they all shared a playful banter, Grace noticed James glancing their way. *I'll deal with him later.*

Edward suddenly concluded, upon seeing Grace at Dani's house, that this must be the woman James was interested in. There was a silent energy between them. As long as they weren't in any trouble, which was always a gamble with James, Edward liked their chances. *She might be good for him...* He found himself nodding in silent approval.

Dani left Grace in the kitchen and took James' parents to the living room, where they could relax before dinner. They became engrossed in a conversation, but James managed to slip away into the kitchen.

"Hey," James greeted.

"Hi," she answered in a short tone. She had to feel him out. Judging from their last conversation, she wasn't sure how high civility ranked between them.

"How are you?"

"Fine."

"How's the baby?"

"Fine."

"Nylah."

No answer from Grace.

"Grace."

"What."

"Will you at least glance at me?" James implored.

Grace had been avoiding eye contact with him. "Why?"

"Please, Nylah."

Grace felt a slight tug in her heart and she lifted her eyes to meet his light brown ones; they provided the perfect contrast with his dark brown complexion.

"Are you going to give me more than one-word answers?"

Grace smiled slightly, trying to decide between her tough resolve and having a pleasant day. "Maybe," she said in jest.

James smiled at her. "Are you going to be mean to me all day today?"

His smile... it always made her insides flip around. Grace started to tell him she hadn't been mean, but that wasn't completely true. "Why shouldn't I be? You deserve every bit of it."

James held up his hands in apologetic agreement. "No argument here. I do deserve it. But it's Thanksgiving—your favorite."

Grace softened. She didn't want to be mad at him. By now they had figured out that they brought out the best and the worst in each other. She couldn't resist smiling at him fully this time. "Fine," she conceded. "Truce," she said, offering her hand. "Today we will have a good day."

He took it and stepped closer to her. "That's my girl," he whispered, pulling her into a hug.

Grace could have melted in his arms, they felt so good. She was actually grateful to have this private moment with James today. It meant more than she thought it could.

James pulled away but stayed right in front of her. "I'm sorry about how I carried on the last time we spoke. I don't ever want to have a conversation like that with you again. I was ashamed of my actions and I've been waiting for the right opportunity to apologize. I hope you can accept."

"I do accept, thank you. And I owe you an apology, as well. I handled the situation poorly and if we can manage, I'd like the same."

They sealed their apology with a simple kiss. Now that they had come to a mutual agreement about their prior interaction, there was something else they needed to discuss.

"I thanked Nathan for his offer, but I told him I wouldn't be able to accept," Grace offered. Better for her to bring it up than James.

James was silent as he went and sat at the counter. "How did he take it?" he curiously asked.

Grace sat next to him. They turned to face each other. "Not well. We didn't argue, but... it was a raw conversation for him. He said that if we were to marry, he would necessitate that I tell him who the father of my child was. His request was perfectly reasonable, but I told him I wouldn't do that and he became upset. He insisted, but I plainly expressed that he would never know unless the father and I decided to disclose that information. That's when we both realized that there are areas lacking in trust, for one reason or another. It's not fair to get into a relationship with him and he doesn't have my complete trust."

James took her hands in his. "Is that the only reason you turned him down?"

"No," Grace answered. She felt herself gripping his hands tighter. "You were right—I need to be with someone I love. And I don't love him. My heart belongs to you... I can't help it. I realize that everything hurts so badly with you because I still love you."

James sighed. "I don't know what to say—there is nothing I *can* say that will make any of this better. It's all in my actions. I'm working it out. Even though this distance between us has been agonizing, it has given me great opportunity for reflection... among other things."

They sat there, fingers intertwined, relishing the peaceful silence between them. It had been a while since they had been able to do this. After a few minutes, James brought Grace's hands to his lips and kissed them softly. That was one of the most endearingly affectionate gestures he'd done with her. Then he stood, gently kissed her on the lips and said, "Come on. Let's go find the others."

He was taking them to neutral territory so that they

wouldn't venture into tempting territory. It was the first time he had ever been the one to initiate a "safe place" and it didn't go unnoticed by Grace.

They were hand in hand until they were close enough to see and be seen by the others; then they let go.

Upon their entrance, Dani smiled and asked, "Well, is everybody ready to eat?"

Dinner was wonderful. James sat next to Grace on one side of the table, his parents sat next to each other on the opposite side and Dani and Lawrence sat at opposite heads of the table. There was light-hearted, humorous conversation between everybody. Grace ate to her heart's content, savoring every single bite of food. They all ate as much as they wanted, till they were finished. They continued with conversation while Lawrence helped Dani clear the table and bring out dessert and coffee... herbal tea with honey for Grace.

As they settled down from dinner, Katherine focused her attention on Grace with a question.

"Grace honey, I've noticed that there is sadness in your eyes. Even though there is a glow in your face, you don't seem internally happy. Is everything all right?"

The table became quiet. There was an immediate air of uncomfortableness, not knowing how Grace would respond.

I have really got to do something about this 'sadness' in my eyes. Grace was not surprised at the forward accuracy of Katherine's question, but she was mildly surprised to find that she wanted to answer as directly as possible.

All eyes were on Grace as she struggled with where to begin. She decided to start in general terms and go from there.

"Everything has not been all right with me for a while. I'm afraid I allowed myself to willingly participate in a lifestyle not conducive to my spirit. I am now dealing with the repercussions."

"What has happened to you, honey?"

Grace smiled into a solemn grimace. "I'm pregnant. That should explain everything, you see."

Katherine reached her hand across the table, seeking to comfort her.

Meanwhile, Grace's declaration sounded a very loud alarm in Edward's ear. He immediately, but subtly shifted his gaze from Grace to James. *Please tell me this is not his child.* He recalled the energy from earlier that he had sensed between James and Grace, but he figured it was due to a mutual interest... not a hidden pregnancy.

The rest were tuned in to Grace as she told parts of her story, carefully leaving out any information about the father.

Edward cleared his throat. "So, what about the child's father?"

"I'm sorry, but what about him?" Grace asked.

"I couldn't help but notice he is mysteriously absent from your story."

Grace tried to think of the best words possible, as to not implicate James. "Um, we're on speaking terms, somewhat, but he's not an active part of our lives right now."

"Is this distance by your choice, or his?" Edward asked. That would weigh in on one aspect of this situation.

"Well... it was ultimately my decision... predicated by some other things that have happened. It was the best choice for me at the time."

"So were you dating and perhaps got carried away, or was your relationship intentionally physical, by choice?" he asked.

Grace flushed deeply at the question. Glancing around at the others, she was acutely aware of James' disposition. "Umm..."

"Grace," Katherine cut in, "please excuse my husband. He is sometimes not aware that his questions can become too personal." Katherine made sure her manner told her husband to stop interrogating Grace.

"I apologize, Grace. It's none of my business, and it's certainly not my intention to upset or embarrass you. I guess

I'm just trying to understand this man's logic. Hopefully, he will come to his senses for the sake of you and the child you share."

James clenched his jaw, but showed no emotion. He refused to acknowledge his father, enough to confirm Edward's suspicions.

Edward leaned back in his chair and sighed heavily. *I cannot believe he has done this.*

Katherine tossed her cloth napkin on the table, pushed back in her chair and said, "Grace, if you don't mind, I'd like to talk to you in private. Dani can come too if she'd like and if it's okay with you."

Grace nodded and the women went to Dani's bedroom.

The gentlemen stayed at the table. Lawrence left to take dishes to the kitchen.

Finally, James turned to his father.

Edward's eyes bore into James. "Do you know who her child's father is?" Edward asked.

"Yes. As her pastor, we have discussed the situation."

You don't know because you're her pastor, you know because it's you. Edward was certain his gut was right and it would be addressed with the both of them later on. Now was not the right time to lay into James, but it would be done.

"Do the other two know? Dani and Lawrence?"

"No, she hasn't told them."

Nor have you. The wheels in Edward's mind were turning even after Lawrence came back to the table and the conversation shifted from Grace to other things. He had so many questions for James and he was determined to get answers.

****

The ladies sat in the sitting area in Dani's bedroom, in close proximity to each other. Katherine and Grace were deep in conversation.

"One thing I now know by experience is that when you start out with little allowances, you always tell yourself you can keep it controlled." Grace found that her emotions were still up and down, and could change in a split second. She had been okay out in the dining room, but once they sat in Dani's room, she couldn't stop her tears from falling as she and Katherine continued. "But you're never in control when you willingly participate in sin. I kept telling myself we would get it right, but it never happened."

"Were you coerced into anything?"

Grace sniffled with surprise. "No ma'am, not at all. It is safe to say that he planned to woo me, which led to a proposition. Ultimately, it was my choice. I could have put a stop to it at any time, but I never did."

"I sense that all is not completely over with this man. You need to be careful Grace, and choose the right path."

"I'm really trying," Grace whispered. "It's hard for me to resist him. He's been adhering to my boundaries, but there's this draw between us that goes beyond the baby. My being pregnant has only complicated and intensified our feelings. Everything's such a mess."

Katherine felt her heart breaking, not only for Grace, but for all the other women who allowed themselves to get caught up in sinful behavior. She felt strongly concerned for Grace—maybe because she believed James was involved somehow.

"How do you feel, having to now go through restoration, dear?"

"I'm ashamed of myself. It's like I'm split in two though. The one side that is desperately trying to get myself spiritually correct... and the other side that just wants to be with him. Good or bad, right or wrong."

"That's a very dangerous place to be, Grace."

"I know," Grace acknowledged, tears falling to her dress. "I haven't been able to verbalize that before. I don't know what to do. I don't know how to handle this at all. It has been excruciating for me. I know it's my fault..."

"You're not only to blame. But you have to stay strong

and on the right path. It's the only way for you to properly heal and be delivered."

They continued to talk some more, Lady Garrison offering gentle wisdom and Dani offering gentle friendship. They prayed with and for Grace that she would be granted God's guidance and strength. *Please God, help me to make it.*

As the evening wound down, Grace was tired. *Time to go home.* Grace expressed her thanks and said her goodnights. Dani was preparing to escort her outside, but James came up to them smiling.

"Hey Dani, I got it."

Dani backed off, smiling at the both of them getting along.

Edward glared at his son, shaking his head.

Once they were outside, Grace linked her arm through his as they made their way in silence. Her car was parked in the driveway, on the side of the house. Grace repositioned herself to lean her back up against the car when they reached it.

"Thank you," she said, turning to him.

"You're welcome," he smiled. He leaned in close to her and kissed her temple, inhaling her scent. Her fragrance was a light fresh scent. James loved it.

"I miss you," James said. "Will you allow me to come over later?"

"Why not? It's Thanksgiving after all," Grace smiled in reply. *I'm letting down all my defenses. I've worked hard for the boundaries I've set with him and now I'm allowing them to just disappear. Since I know that I cannot resist him, I shouldn't let him come… but I really want to see him. Nothing has to happen…*

They came together for what was to be a brief kiss, but turned into a deep, searching, scorching kiss. *Well, almost nothing.*

"I'll try not to keep you waiting long," he told her. Just as he was about to help her in the car, he stopped suddenly, seemingly paralyzed.

"What is it?" Grace asked. She noticed him staring down and they both realized that he had subconsciously placed his hand on her belly and the baby moved. Grace smiled, placing her hand over his.

"The baby," James whispered.

"Pretty amazing, isn't it?" Grace replied.

"It's incredible," James responded.

After a few quiet moments, he helped her into her car and closed the door.

She rolled down her window. "Call me when you get to my place, in case I've dozed off." She pulled off just after he leaned in for another kiss.

James and his parents left Dani and Lawrence's home a little while after that. He took them back to his house, told them he'd be back later and left before they could interrogate him.

When James pulled into Grace's complex, he called her as she'd requested. "Hey, Nylah. I'm here."

"Okay. I'll unlock the door for you."

He was up in what seemed like seconds, locking the door behind him.

Casting an eye over Grace resting on the couch, he tried to restrain from going straight to her and holding her.

"Are you okay?" he asked.

She smiled brightly at him. "I'm just tired. And sore."

He sat next to her and pulled her legs across his lap. He gently massaged them as he talked to her. "Why are you sore? Haven't you been taking it easy?"

"Yes sir, I have been taking it easy." She laughed when he made a face at her. "I'm sore because my body is changing and trying to adjust."

James took in a quick breath at the mention of her body changing. He wondered in what ways. Clearing his throat, he asked, "In what ways?"

"Well, I'm almost six months now, so of course my stomach is growing a bit more round. My legs are tight, as you can feel, my back hurts sometimes and my—" Grace paused, glancing at James, "—my...uh, my upper region," Grace said motioning, not wanting to actually say the word, "is really tender and slightly bigger." Grace sat up and moved her legs, feeling flushed all over.

James stared at her for a few moments before he moved to sit behind her. Stretching out his legs on both sides of her, he laid back and pulled her down gently to lie against him. He kissed the top of her head and massaged her scalp.

After a few quiet minutes, James said, "I think my dad knows. I'm certain he strongly suspects, but he hasn't had a chance to ask me directly."

Grace slightly turned. "Was it because of what I said? I wasn't trying to implicate you..."

"Sshhh. I know you weren't. This is on me. It was only a matter of time before they found out anyway."

Grace started to rise, but James pulled her back down. "Are you going to tell him?" Grace asked.

"Yes, especially if he asks me directly. Regardless, I would need to tell both him and my mom. They don't need to find out any other way."

"Do you want me to be with you when you tell them?"

She was so considerate... even after everything he had done to her. He realized he still had a lot to learn about love. Grace loved him without conditions. He had not done so well reciprocating and needed to change that.

"No, baby. I need to do it myself. But thank you for offering. I can't even begin to explain what that means to me... or what you mean to me."

"Don't get all sentimental on me right now. I might actually start to believe you."

They both knew she was kidding, but the words struck a chord in James. His actions had done so much damage to their relationship that maybe a part of her honestly felt like he didn't care about her.

He sat them up slowly and came around her again to face

her. He traced her features, trying to figure out the right words to say.

Almost as if she could read his thoughts, she said, "James, I know you love me."

"Do you? I haven't done well showing it."

"No, you haven't," she agreed. "But our feelings are real, despite our circumstance. I can't discount yours anymore than I can my own."

"I need you, Nylah. Please don't give up on me yet."

Grace reached up to his face. "I'll see what I can do," she smiled.

James leaned down to give her a kiss. They slowly leaned back onto the couch. They broke the kiss, each struggling for breath.

"We shouldn't be doing this—" Grace said.

"—I should go," James said at the same time.

They contemplated their words, neither making an effort to move. Grace first noticed that this was the second time in a day that James offered to cut off the temptation. That intrigued her psyche... and her desire for him. She then noted that her body was relaxed underneath him. She finally realized he was gently massaging where she was sore and it felt good.

"Does this hurt?" he murmured.

"No," Grace replied in a raspy whisper.

"We're supposed to be married by now. I can't help but think about you every single night, wondering when we can be together for good. I know we're separated because of my actions, among other things. I'm sorry, Nylah... I'm really sorry."

He kissed her again and again, each time taking them closer to a point of no return. They eventually did what they should not have done; both overcome with a blazing and familiar passion.

"I'm sorry," James croaked out, his eyes filled with guilt. "I—I can't keep doing this to you."

Grace just nodded, too shaken to speak, in silent disbelief that she had allowed herself to, once again, give in to temptation.

They both got up and put their clothes on. Grace turned to James. *He has never apologized before. He actually seems sorry.* She silently strode to him and allowed him to encircle her waist and kiss her palm as she kissed his shoulder, studying his eyes.

They sat back down, thinking through the silence. Ever trying to be the voice of reason, Grace finally said, "We have to figure out what we're going to do if we can't keep our hands to ourselves. Because this won't work."

"I know. I didn't intend for this to happen; I just wanted to come see you. Hopefully, I have compromised you for the last time," he said.

They talked a little while longer, reinstating some necessary boundaries and initializing a new mode of communication. They embraced for a while before he left.

James spent his drive home feeling ridiculous emotions. This was the first time he and Grace had ever been intimate and one of them left afterwards; before, they had always spent the night together. He felt a longing tugging at him, knowing he needed to do his part to fix this, so he would not have to leave her anymore.

He stepped into his house around 2 A.M., to find his father waiting patiently for him. *How fortunate for me,* James thought. *Seems my day of reckoning has come.*

"James," his father said, standing to greet him.

"Dad," James returned.

They stood facing each other. Edward was calm, but there was a glint of anger in his eyes. James was calm also, but he was tired and feeling the sense of irritation he normally got when talking to his father.

"Where have you been this late?" Edward asked.

James dismissed the implication that he needed to answer this particular question by remaining silent.

Edward knew not to ask James open questions like that. "Were you with Grace?"

James didn't *have* to answer that either, but they would dance around the subject until his dad got answers he was satisfied with. "Yes, I was."

His father took that information and let it settle. "You should not be carrying on like this, James."

"I already know that. What else?" That came out harsher than James intended, but at the present moment, he scarcely cared.

"Watch your tone. You are clearly having some issues that you need to deal with appropriately. Staying at Grace's house until early morning is not the appropriate way."

"And you putting your foot down as if I'm a child *is?*" James was getting hot under his collar. These seemed to be the only types of conversations he ever had with his dad.

"Somebody needs to put you in your place, since you refuse to do it yourself!"

"Well, somebody else can do it, then. You're relieved of your entitlement." James started to leave but his father stopped him.

"We're not finished, son." Edward was appalled at James. He didn't understand—this was not how he'd raised him.

James turned around. "I would rather that than to stand here and argue with you. It's not helping either of us."

"Is Grace pregnant with your child?"

James hesitated briefly. He could feel his father teetering on the brink of an explosion. James knew his next words would effectively ignite that explosion. "Yes. Her child is mine."

"What have you been thinking? You're a pastor, James! You have an obligatory duty to uphold biblical standards. Your mother and I did not raise you like this!"

James' frustration broke. "You didn't raise me. Mom did. You were too busy or always gone. The only times I ever seemed to hear from you as a parent was when you criticized me for anything or everything."

"Are you trying to blame me for your predicament? I don't recall making these choices for you. All your mother and I have done is support you."

"I don't know what it is to have your support... I've never known that. I can count on one hand the amount of times you said something remotely along the lines of encouraging me. And I would still have plenty of fingers left."

"James, you are too old for this. This situation with Grace is irresponsible, selfish, clumsy, and unholy. And that's not to mention how you've handled your relationship with her lately. You're not an active part of their *lives*? That is completely unacceptable, as is this entire situation."

"We're working on it," James said, short in tone.

Edward's eyes were hard and his words were like darts. "You'd better find a way to make this right and you had better find it quick. You have compromised yourself in an unimaginable fashion. As one who submits to God's authority, I cannot allow you to remain active in your position. I'll give you a small window of time to figure out your own way, before I intervene and do it my way," Edward left him with those words.

Nothing short of what James had expected, his message was clear and concise. His father's ultimatum was only shades milder than what he thought he had coming. And he still saw the same disappointment in his dad's eyes, only to a greater measure. The same disappointment that never ceased to make James feel like a failure.

Chapter 16

James woke up to the sound of his father calling his name.
"James. Get up, son. Get dressed. We're leaving in twenty minutes." Then he left.

James glanced at the clock. 7 A.M. *I just managed to fall asleep.* Groaning, he rolled out of bed, irritated that he had been disturbed.

Edward waited for James in the den. He hadn't slept much either, thinking about, not only James' situation, but also about his words. The more he thought about it, the more he realized that he and James had not shared a meaningful conversation... ever. Every talk he could recall, ended up with one of them upset with the other and nothing ever resolved.

All this time he hadn't given much thought to the state of his relationship with James. In all of his counseling with other families about brokenness amongst families, he had never considered his own relationship that needed repairing. It was an unsettling realization. One that needed to be rectified. He heard his wife's voice in his head, chastising him for ignoring her warnings about his relationship with James.

James appeared in twenty minutes exactly, while Edward was in the midst of his thoughts.

"Where's Mom?" James asked.

"She's resting. She's not coming with us," Edward answered.

"Are we meeting with someone?" James was skeptical about this whole morning outing.

"No son, we're going alone. Just the two of us."

Alone? Like a father/son outing? What is going on? James didn't know what to think or expect, but he felt an inward push to go along with it and find out.

They arrived at a restaurant and were seated in a semi-private area. After they ordered breakfast, James broke the silence.

"Dad, what are we here for?" James asked.

"Well first, I'd like to acknowledge that my position remains the same. You've had time to handle this and since it has not been taken care of, your grace period—no pun intended—is over. If you're willing to do it, you must be willing to face it."

"You brought me here to tell me this? We could have just gone another round at the house and called it a day."

Edward held up his hand to silence James. "Easy. That's not all I want to discuss with you."

James felt exasperation all around him. *What now?*

"I want to talk to you and Grace, together."

James knew he had no choice but to agree. "Yes, sir."

Edward continued. "I'd also like to talk about what you said to me during our argument." After a brief pause, Edward earnestly questioned James. "Do you honestly feel like I didn't raise you?"

James suspended his thoughts. He hadn't expected this turn in the conversation. He didn't even think his father had taken his words seriously. "Are you sure you want to discuss this here?"

"Neither of us likes to make a public scene. That's one of the things, few they might be, that we have in common. Public may be the best place to at least start."

James was thoughtful before deciding where to begin. "You never came to anything of importance to me, with the exception of my graduations and my wedding. I understood why you were gone, but what I did not, nor have been able to understand, was why we could not seem to get along. Couple that with my everlasting frustration that nothing I did ever pleased you and you have the makings of a seriously strained relationship."

Edward raised his brows slightly. "Why am I just now hearing about this?"

"This isn't exactly something I care to bring up out of the blue. But if you think about it, we've never had a healthy conversation. I know that we may not always agree but contrary to whatever you may think, the last thing I want is to argue with you for the rest of our lives."

Edward was... surprised. He had to admit inwardly that he knew James intuitively well, but not relationally well between father and son. He had usually known when James had done something wrong—he could sense it—and those were the times when he took to interacting with him. It had not dawned on him to fill in the blanks around those times. Once again, he recalled his wife's voice in the back of his mind, warning him that he needed to work on his relationship with James. He thought he had done well to provide correction and guidance, not realizing that he had not done well to offer moral support and encouragement.

"My verbal interaction with you over the years may have been harsh," Edward started slowly, "but I have only wanted you to put your best foot forward and succeed in life."

"Dad, I get that... now. It took me a while, but I have finally been able to see that. That, however, is not the point."

"You don't feel I have been there for you as a father

should?"

"Do you feel that you have?"

Edward relented. "I'm sorry, son. In some ways, yes, but in important ways, no."

James had never realized what hearing that admission from his father would do for him. He certainly had never considered that his dad would apologize for it. But here they were, and he had just received both... he felt that a heavy weight had lifted. True, he was far too old to blame anything he'd done on anybody else. Still, it helped to feel validated by his parents.

James sensed a turning point. His father was trying, so he would too. Besides, if Grace could forgive him, he could certainly forgive his father. He loved him, after all.

"Dad, I don't want to hold onto any of this. I would like for us to work toward a better relationship. I know you love me." James paused, hearing Grace's words. *James, I know you love me.* He was in no position to harbor ill will. "I would just appreciate it if you showed it a little differently sometimes."

"I'll be more in tune to how I deal with you. And yes, I do love you, son. Even though now may not be one of those times, understand that I have certainly been proud of you."

James nodded in acknowledgement. He knew his father's words were sincere and that was a good starting point for them.

"Now listen, son; about your current matter... you do understand why it is necessary for me to take a hard line with you, don't you?"

"I wouldn't expect anything less from you. Did you tell Mom?"

"Yes, your mother and I spoke this morning."

"How did she take it?" James was always worried about hurting his mother. He knew she'd be disappointed.

"Your mother is strong. She suspected, as I did, and she's disappointed, as I am, but we'll all get through this. We're not going to abandon you. Nor will we abandon Grace now. And speaking in terms of abandoning Grace, do you care to explain yourself?" His father had taken a stern glare to James.

James felt the shame about how he'd dealt with Grace and her pregnancy. He swallowed hard. "I didn't mean to abandon her. And I know my actions don't concur with that statement." James knew he should just tell it all. He'd been holding it in too long, not being able to talk to anybody... or almost anybody. *It's time to come clean.* James told his father the complete story, from start to present.

"James you can't do this to her. You need to get right with God, for your sake and the sake of your family."

After breakfast, the men arrived back at James' house to find Grace there talking to Katherine.

"It's good to see you, Grace," Edward said. "I'm glad you're here. I told James I wanted to talk to the both of you, so we'll get right to it."

They all sat in the living room discussing the particulars of their situation.

"The both of you already know that we are hurt and disappointed that you have allowed this to happen, considering your positions at the church. We expected better of you, as does God. It puts us in a very precarious situation, which adds frustration and anger to the process," Edward chastised.

"With that said, let's lay some ground rules for you two, since your judgment concerning each other is not always sound."

James interrupted his father. "We already have boundaries in place, dad. We reestablished those last night."

"You mean this morning. To which bears my point. I'm not trying to control you; I'm well aware that you are both adults and I cannot police your life. But it will not be said of your mother and I that we let you carry on despite knowledge of the situation."

Pausing to see if either of them was going to object again, Edward continued. "You are not to be alone in each other's house. Period. No exceptions. Do you understand?"

"Yes, sir," they both answered.

"Now, Grace," Edward said, "I've been fairly easy on you, mainly because I was so upset with James, but I know that neither of you are blameless. This is one-half your fault, and the truth is, it doesn't matter how many times you told James how wrong you both were. You still continued with the relationship as much as he did. I guess I can acknowledge that you've tried to make progress without James, but I honestly can't give you much praise. The only reason any of this has come to light is because of your pregnancy. It is my belief that the both of you would have hidden every part of your relationship if you could have and gotten away with it. God is not pleased and He has decided that it's time for this to stop."

Grace took her rebuke—not that she had much choice in the matter. There wasn't anything she could say in her defense.

"James," his father said, "you have two weeks maximum to handle this on your own. Otherwise, I will handle as I see fit."

James nodded in concession. It was almost a relief though. He needed some structure and his father was providing that.

"Regarding your relationship," Katherine added, "either you're going to be together or you're not. And if you decide to be together, that means marriage, not just being together, as you have previously carried on. Some definite decisions need to be made by the both of you."

"There are also the matters concerning your character and integrity," Edward picked back up. "It's shot. You may be able to recover it, but it won't happen overnight. They've had a little more time to deal with you Grace, but that process is almost going to start all over once they find out you've been with James.

"And James, they're going to be exceptionally hurt and angry with you. Not only was your relationship sneaky, it makes you seem careless for not coming clean when Grace did.

"There may even be talk of dismissing you as pastor, and rightfully so. Ultimately, whatever they decide, you will handle yourself with as much integrity as possible."

James knew the possible consequences early on, but what he had not really considered was losing the church. Now that it may be too late, he realized that he didn't want that to happen.

"Everyone will have to deal patiently with each other," Katherine said. "It's going to be tough, but you knew this going in, so now it must be dealt with."

"Should you decide to not get married, you have to figure out visitation and everything else that comes with raising a child in separate households. You'll also have to consider how the situation will be dealt with should either or both of you marry other people. There is much to consider and work out, so you have no time for further foolishness," Edward finished sternly.

"We love the both of you very much," Katherine expressed. "We are constantly praying for you and we're here for you."

"Since we're all together, I'd like to pray for the both of you," Edward said.

After the prayer was concluded, James observed Grace wiping her eyes. He squeezed her hand, trying to reassure her that they would fully find their way back to God.

****

Later that evening, James answered his phone to a shrill voice. He held it away from his ear until he could decipher words.

"James! James are you there?"

"Yes, Michelle, I'm here. Hopefully I still have my hearing. Let me guess—"

"Yes, Dad told me about your ridiculousness. You got her pregnant?! What is the matter with you?"

James rolled his eyes. "Michelle, please—"

"Don't even. Have you lost your mind? You're a pastor, bighead! Behavior not becoming of such."

"Do you not think I haven't heard all of this already? Surely you know our father."

"If I was in any position to come and beat you up, I certainly would. You are so lucky right now."

"Whatever, Michelle. Don't put your holiness on a pedestal like you've never had to repent."

"Do you know how stupid you sound right now? You've been involved with her for almost a year, and knowing you, it's been without any thoughts of repentance. At least I came to my senses, so God could help me."

James sighed, not feeling like hearing Michelle go off on him.

"Oh, you can huff and puff all you want."

James groaned. "Michelle…"

"You are full of so much foolishness right now, I'm sure I could accurately guess every stage you've gone through since she told you about the baby. You had better make sure nothing happens to them."

"Speaking of responsibilities, did you ever tell Mom and Dad about your—"

"Shut up, James. That is not relevant to this conversation."

"The only difference is that I got caught in mine. Don't you ever forget when you're talking to me, that you have dirt swept under your rug."

"I can't believe you would say that to me," Michelle faintly said. "You need to handle yourself better."

James started to feel bad about his outburst, but Michelle didn't give him the chance to apologize.

"I don't want to talk to you anymore right now, but this is not over. It won't be over for a long time. Goodbye."

James heard a light sniff before she clicked off the phone.

James sighed. He knew she was right. He should not have

gotten mad at her calling him out. He deserved that, at the very least. He decided to send her a text:

James: Hey Chelle. I'm sorry for what I said. I was out of line.

He didn't know if she would respond, or if she was too upset to deal with him right now. His phone buzzed a few minutes later.

Michelle: Just don't do it again. Bighead.

James smiled. They were all right.

Chapter 17

Grace pulled up to a corner store and waited for Emma to get in. The young girl was, not surprisingly, quiet but also visibly shaken. Grace waited a few moments before opening up their conversation.

"Emma... why are you over here? And have you called your mother? Does she know what's going on?"

Emma shook her head. "I haven't talked to her yet," she whispered. Turning to Grace, she promised, "I will. I will. I just couldn't call her first. Sometimes I can't talk to her about stuff; she'll go crazy."

"Honey, she worries about you. Not to be a nuisance, but because she loves you. She won't be happy that you called me first."

"Well, thank you for coming."

"I'm not just going to leave you here if you're in trouble. But you need to talk to your mom. And you'll have to tell her you called me first."

"Yes, ma'am," Emma said.

They rode together for a few silent minutes. Grace noticed Emma wiping her face.

"Are you ready to talk?" Grace gently asked Emma.

After a long breath, Emma began. "It all kind of started a few weeks ago. I was at school and this guy came over to our lunch table. He's a *senior*, Grace. Very cute—very popular. Anyways, he seemed to take an interest in me; of course I was flattered. One day he asked me to meet him in the library during our free period; he must have been playing on my interest in books. He would give me compliments, sit with me at lunch, all sorts of stuff. It was cool. He liked me for me... or, at least I thought he did. So, today we had early out. He asked if we—me and Kiana—wanted to go to the café with his friend. We said yes but that afterward, we would have to go home."

Grace broke in. "You went to the café with him without supervision?"

"Yes. I know I wasn't supposed to. But I didn't think anything would happen."

That makes two of us... "So what happened next?" Grace asked.

"At the café, we sat in these booths. Kiana and his friend on one side, and he sat next to me on the other. He put his arm around me and I didn't tell him to move it. I think I figured that since he was paying attention to me that it was okay to be flirty with him. After we ate, he asked me if I was sure I had to go straight home. He said we could go back to his house and watch a movie and then he could take me home. I told him I couldn't be alone with him, but he said his mom would be there, so everything would be fine."

"Oh, Emma."

"I know. I said okay, and Kiana asked me if I was sure. She went home and I left with him. We get to his house and he puts on a movie. I asked where his mom was and he said, 'Oh, I forgot; she's out of town.' I start getting real uncomfortable but he says for me to relax so we can watch the movie. I thought just watching would be harmless. Wrong. He starts rubbing my thigh and then trying to kiss my neck. I move away and tell him to stop. He comes back over and tries to kiss me for real. I'm not having it and I tell him to take me home."

"Was he upset when you told him that?"

"He wouldn't listen to me and said if I didn't want to have sex with him, then I wouldn't have come to his house. I told him if he were any decent kind of guy, he wouldn't have lied to me about his mom being home. He tried to grab my wrists, but I pulled away and socked him across his face. Then I told him I was serious and he needed to take me home right then. He finally said okay, but there was this cold look in his eyes. He pulled into that corner store and told me to get out. I eyeball him all crazy and tell him to take me home like I'd said. He reaches across me, opens the door and said if I didn't get out, he's going to push me out. So I got out, he drove off, and then I called you. Why Grace? Why did any of this have to happen?"

"Sometimes, when we're disobedient, things happen in a way that we may not always understand. That's why we have to try to keep ourselves right. Obedience is of the utmost importance."

"Is that what happened to you?" Emma inquired. "You were disobedient?"

"Emma, I've made a lot of mistakes—disobedience being only one of many. I can tell you from personal experience that it is definitely a road you don't want to travel. Seems like you now may have a personal experience of your own that tells you the same thing."

Emma was thoughtful. "Grace, you're pregnant right?"

"Yes, I am," Grace answered. She felt her phone vibrate and quickly glanced to see who was calling. *James. Of course, it is... I'll call him back later.*

"What about your baby's dad? Is he with you? Does he love you?" she asked curiously. "I mean, would he do something to you like what this guy did to me?"

Grace briefly reflected on everything that had transpired

between her and James after she told him she was pregnant. "Listen honey, we're not going to talk about him right now. I just want you to see my situation clearly. You don't want to end up like me." Grace had tears in her eyes. *This is not a conversation I ever anticipated having. Shame on me.*

"I know we haven't spent much time together lately—I miss it. It's not fair that Mom made me stop talking to you."

"Your mother is looking out for what's best for you. It's her duty as a parent to put whatever boundaries in place that she feels are necessary. Just because you may not agree, does not mean that you have the right to challenge her about it."

"She's such a hypocrite," Emma said bitterly. "She acts like she has such a problem with you now, but she's been in the same predicament before. If I end up like that, it will be because of her example, not yours."

"Emma honey, don't be upset with your mom."

"Why not? She always wants her point to be made, but she won't listen to any of mine. I don't try to disrespect her. Sometimes she's just really frustrating. She's not perfect, yet she says negative things about your situation all the time."

Grace wasn't quite sure how to take that. She knew Lisa had been mad at her, but she hadn't expected Lisa to bad mouth her to Emma.

"Listen to me, Emma. You're smart, sweet, and have so much promise for your life. Learn from our mistakes and don't repeat." Grace exhaled deeply, sad that in her predicament, she was advising her young friend on making mistakes. "Just maintain your focus on what matters. You'll have plenty of time for other stuff later." Grace turned to glance at Emma, seeing concern gloss her face.

"Grace, watch out!" Emma cried.

Grace turned back to the road with immediate panic. She hadn't noticed until it was too late that a car was approaching them, coming into her lane. She couldn't swerve into the next lane because there were other cars in it. The racing car clipped the front of Grace's, sending them into a tailspin, hitting at least two other cars.

Grace screamed, "Jesus!" as her car turned and hit another car. That hit sent them in the direction of a large pole. She heard Emma screaming, and all she could think was, *please God, don't let Emma get hurt. Let us all be okay.*

They were approaching the pole head on. They were going to hit it; it couldn't be avoided. Grace determined that she had to do everything possible to diminish the impact for Emma. She was able to manage enough control over the car to quickly turn it so that they would slam into the pole only on her side of the car.

Grace tried to brace for the impact but it still felt unreal. She didn't know what she hit her head on but she saw a bright flash of lights before painfully realizing she couldn't move. She barely heard Emma calling her name.

"Emma... you okay?" It hurt for Grace to talk, and she didn't have enough strength to observe her, but she had to ask and make sure Emma was okay.

"Yes Grace, I'm fine. Please keep talking to me," Emma pleaded. "I'm calling 911," she said, fumbling for her phone. Emma saw Grace bleeding from her head, but nowhere else. She was scared for her because Grace couldn't keep her eyes open and her body was cramped in her seat.

"The baby," Grace managed to whisper, feeling her body about to give out. "Make... sure they... they save baby," she finished. Grace could barely hear Emma calling out to her, but those calls became fainter and fainter until Grace completely blacked out.

"GRACE!" Emma screamed. Grace had stopped talking and had gone completely limp. "Grace, please open your eyes," she pleaded. "Please, answer me. GRACE!!" Hysterically, Emma got out of the car as several other people who witnessed the accident came to help them.

"Please, help us! She's not conscious. She can't die!" Emma cried.

"Don't worry, honey," a woman said. "We saw the whole

thing and we called EMS already. We're going to help your mom."

"She's not my mom. Please… she can't move. She's not talking anymore. We have to get her out! She's pregnant—we have to help her!" Emma sobbed.

Another lady came and stood by Emma as they watched some men try to pry Grace's door open. The women tried to console Emma, but she was too emotionally distressed. EMS arrived in about two minutes, the fire truck right behind them. Emma started shouting for them to get Grace out.

"She's pregnant! You have to save her and the baby!" Emma was weeping, as she watched them pry the car door away and carefully remove Grace. They came to her and said they needed to check her out and that she would have to go with them to the hospital. She held Grace's hand all the way to the hospital, crying and pleading for her to wake up—praying for her to be okay.

Chapter 18

James sat, reflecting on the past several days. Many things had transpired, some good, one not. He felt a continuous relief at having to finally do what was right. He wasn't sure though, how he was going to let everything out. By now, he had little more than a week left to figure it out.

And there will be consequences... James jolted at the memory of God's warning to him. What kind of consequences? James was worried about that. He wasn't sure what it meant. He knew sin had consequences and not all were the same. The thought made him sick. All he could do was pray for mercy.

James called Grace; it went to her voicemail again. Hopefully she wasn't avoiding him. They had an intense discussion the day before about their relationship. He asked her if she'd thought again about being with someone else. He wanted to promise that they wouldn't be with other people, but she told him that until he told the church about his involvement with her, nothing would be discussed between them. He was frustrated, but she shrugged it off. She reminded him that his time was running out. She also warned him that if he wasn't man enough to confess on his own, she would definitely have to figure out his place in her life.

James decided that he would start by telling Lawrence, since he was the assistant pastor. That would be difficult enough, but it was necessary. James grabbed his keys and started to leave when his phone rang. Maybe Grace was calling him back. Instead, he saw an unrecognized number. He curiously answered the phone.

"Hello?"

"Hello, may I speak with James Garrison please?"

"Speaking."

"Mr. Garrison, this is Connie at Brighton Memorial Hospital. You're listed as an emergency contact for Ms. Nylah Anderson."

James' heartbeat intensified greatly. "What happened to Nylah?" he asked.

"Ms. Anderson was in a car accident…"

James slowly sank to the chair, feeling a surge of emotional and dazed bewilderment as the nurse told him about Grace's injuries. He tried to maintain a coherent state, but all he could make out were 'head injury', 'unconscious', and 'coma'.

"She's—she's pregnant. What about the baby?" James asked.

"I don't have any information about the baby at this time." The nurse gave him Nylah's room number.

James blurted out, "I'll be right there."

He shook his head a few times, furiously so, and drove as fast as he could to the hospital. He raced to the nurses' station to obtain more information before going to Grace's room. They informed him that they also tried calling Danielle Walters, but was unable to reach her, and that's when they called James. They still didn't have an update on the baby, but promised him one as soon as possible.

James asked if anybody else had been hurt in the accident. They told him the other passenger had not been hurt, and had been picked up by the parents.

James quickly found Grace's ICU room, pausing before opening the door. He slowly stepped in, inhaling a heavy breath at the site of Grace. His eyes watered and his chest tightened seeing the amount of tubes hooked up to her, all the machines to monitor her. He struggled to fight back tears while standing over her, observing as much of her as he could from head to toe. Her forehead was swollen, close to where she had a medium-sized gash right at her hairline. There were no other scrapes on her body. James noticed a few bruises and wondered where else she had them. He wondered how much pain she was in. He wondered about the baby.

James gently kissed her forehead and sat next to her bed. He took her hand and spoke, hoping she could hear him. "Nylah. Baby, I'm so sorry. I'm sorry this has happened to you. I'm sorry for everything," he lamented, stroking her hand. "Please, wake up, baby. I need you. I know... that's pretty selfish of me. So, I would appreciate it if you woke up to tell me just how selfish you think it is. Tell me how wrong I've been. Tell me you still love me, you just don't like me sometimes. Tell me whatever you want... I just want to hear your voice."

James felt his tears push over the edges of his swollen eyes. There was no way he would be able to take losing her and the baby—not like this. "The doctors will check you out in a few, to make sure the baby is all right. If he or she is anything like its mother, the both of you will be just fine." James paused before adding with a quiet urgency, "You have to be. You have to be okay."

James sat in silence, stroking Grace's hand, thinking about all they'd been through. He loved her, but he had consistently made bad choices in her regard. If he could rectify that in any way, he silently vowed that he would.

He went between talking to her, to praying, to silently wondering about various aspects of their relationship, before and now. While he was thinking, Dani and Lawrence came in.

"Oh, my God. Gracie?" Dani mused, rushing over to the other side of her bed. "How did this happen to you?" she said to herself as she canvassed over Grace carefully.

A sympathetic Lawrence came beside James. They briefly greeted before he went over to comfort Dani.

"We came as soon as I got the message," Dani assured. "They called you, too?" she addressed James, but didn't take her eyes off of Grace.

James nodded. "Only after they couldn't reach you. I was next on her emergency contact list." James explained to them what the nurse told him about Grace's condition.

Dani closed her eyes, wiping her falling tears. "What about the baby?" she asked, trying to register this information.

"They don't know. Not yet, anyway."

"You don't have to stay," Dani told him, still focused on Grace. "I know your relationship with her has been different since you found out about the baby. I'll tell her you came when she wakes up."

James clenched his jaw. "I'm not leaving her. Not again. Especially not when she's like this." He took Grace's hand in his.

"Really James, you don't have—"

"No, Dani. I said I'm not leaving her. I can't. I won't do it." James paused before telling them, "I love her."

"Really? Man, we didn't know you felt that strongly," Lawrence said.

After a thorough pause, James heard himself say, "There's a lot you don't know."

"Like what?" Dani asked curiously, finally peeling her gaze away from Grace. She held Grace's other hand, but her attention was now focused on James.

They were briefly interrupted by a nurse. "Excuse me, folks. I wanted to give you all a few minutes with her, but only one person can remain with her at a time."

After she left, James kissed Grace's hand and took a deep breath. *Might as well...* "We'd better talk outside," he said.

He saw their puzzled faces, but they followed him out to the small, private waiting room on the other side of the wall to her room. There was a window that allowed them to view inside her room from where they were.

Once they were all seated, James tried to brace himself for their reaction to what would be an intense revelation for them. "Nylah and I were together before you guys tried to hook us up."

Dani raised her brows at this news. "Come again?"

"We've been together since the end of January."

Dani tilted her head, recalling Grace's words. *It started around the end of January.* Dani shook her thoughts. They were almost two weeks into December. *No, no. This cannot be what Grace told me about. It just can't be.*

"I proposed to her on her birthday and we were supposed to be getting married. Actually, we were supposed to be married by now."

We were supposed to get married. Dani squeezed her eyes, trying to make sense of this. Their stories were already too similar... and that was not a good thing. "No, Gracie was out of town for her birthday," Dani tried to reason. "You were somewhere else."

James smiled ruefully. "I met her there. We were together."

"Together how?" Lawrence asked. He had sat up in his chair, acutely aware of the possible revelations to come and their ramifications.

James swallowed hard. "In the same room. In the same bed."

"Was that the only time you were with her like that?" Lawrence asked.

"No," James solemnly answered. "My intentions in the beginning were to seduce her. We had done some fooling around at first, but we've been sexually intimate since April.

The Sunday right after our first time together," James paused, taking a deep breath, "I propositioned her for a relationship, fully inclusive. She complied. Between both of our homes, we spent almost every week together until September."

Both Dani and Lawrence's eyes grew from dimes to saucers. Lawrence did not like where this story was inevitably leading. Nor could he believe Grace would actually involve herself with James in such a way.

"What!" Dani hissed. Her breathing staggered. Her blood felt like it was simmering.

"Spent together how?" Lawrence firmly asked.

"Essentially living together, day and night." With every piece of revelation, James felt an enormous burden lifting.

We would spend the week together either at my place or his. Dani shook her head as she travelled over to the window to see Grace. *Gracie, how could you?* This was all surprising to Dani... and upsetting. *But you would be surprised. More so than you are right now...* Dani hadn't really thought she would have been any more surprised than when Grace told her about her pregnancy. As it turns out, Grace was right—she knew she would be. She knew Dani would never have suspected James.

Lawrence could see the tension in Dani's body, as he kept a close eye on her. This was not a conversation either of them were expecting. "And her baby?" he asked, stroking his chin. He felt a weighted doom in the pit of his stomach.

James stared Lawrence directly in his eyes and finally let it go. "The baby is mine."

Lawrence covered his eyes with his hand and gripped his head hard. "James..." he groaned.

Dani fumed. She turned furiously, stopping herself from slapping him. "How could you, James? Why would you do something this stupid?"

"I don't have an answer for you. I know it was wrong. That, unfortunately, didn't stop me. It didn't stop either of us."

"Gracie would have been just fine without you interfering

in her life. She, no doubt, would not have chosen to compromise herself with you, if you had just left her alone in the first place," Dani spat at him.

That was true, James had to admit. He had no defense—he hadn't had one since the very beginning.

"James," Lawrence began roughly, "do you know what this is going to do to the church? How do you think they'll react after learning their pastor purposefully slept with his secretary—not once, but for months?"

"I know it's bad..." James said.

"Bad!" Lawrence responded, incredulously. "Aside from this entire situation being sinful and foolishly irresponsible, you've put everyone else in an unstable position, to cater to your selfishness. We defended you, upset that you would be hurt again, now only to find out that you've both been lying to us for almost the entire year."

Lawrence stood and paced around the small space, growling in frustration. "How are any of us supposed to trust you? This is the epitome of hypocrisy." Lawrence's pupils were dilated with fury. "You have the audacity to get up and preach righteousness to the people when you seem to gladly partake in unrighteousness?" He was extremely disappointed in James, to say the least. This situation was catastrophic, at best. At worst... he didn't even want to think about it.

"Wait a minute," Dani started, with a new dawning. "Grace was sat down. *You* sat her down. She had to get in front of the church and apologize. You just sat there and listened to her... and didn't say a word."

James was silently contrite. That instance had remained a sore spot for both he and Grace for a long time. But, they had finally managed to move past it.

"How could you do her like that? Are you really that crass?" Dani angrily asked. "But perhaps, I don't need to ask. We're obviously in this terrible situation because of your carelessness."

"Was her pregnancy intentional?" Lawrence asked. "Or

accidental?"

James sighed and leaned back. Contemplating his answer, he finally said, "Neither." Seeing their irritated faces, he continued. "We discussed having a family, but it was meant to start after we were married. The other side of that story is that we hardly ever used protection…"

"So, the both of you always knew it was possible, but never really considered that it would happen?" Lawrence asked with disgust.

"Yes," James said.

"What is the matter with y'all? You're not teenagers, James. Dare I say that some teenagers would have been far more responsible than the both of you?"

James wished he had done things differently—better. He was becoming more and more sorry that he had ever initiated a relationship with Grace. Well, the wrong kind of relationship, at least. *I really should have married her early on.*

"You don't have anything to say?" Dani sneered.

"None of my words can, or will, make this better."

Lawrence stood, facing him, his hands in his pockets. "You do realize that you must tell the board and the church about this?"

"Yes. I'll discuss that with you a little later."

They were all quiet for a while, until Dani told James quietly, "I want you to leave."

"What? Why? I'm not leaving her, Dani."

"It really shouldn't be a problem for you. You've left her before; you should be able to do it now. Get out." Dani knew she wasn't fighting fair, but none of this was fair and James was the least of her concerns right now.

"Baby, calm down." Lawrence said. "Grace is not completely innocent in this. I know she's your friend—she's our friend, but you have to be able to see it all."

"All I see is this man sitting across from me who decided that he had no problems compromising one of the sisters in the church. You, James, obviously lack fear and reverence for

God. But the least you could've done was not drag someone down with you."

James' face was set tense. "Dani, I know that you're upset, but—"

"This is ALL your fault, James! Leave!"

"Lower your voice," James warned. "You have no right to try—"

"I have no right?" Dani asked incredulously. "You are unbelievable! This is a nightmare, James! Grace *was* innocent. You did this to her! You did it! Do you see her… she's in a coma! She might not wake up. What then?" Dani succumbed to the sobs rising within her. She had just verbalized her worst fears, in a bout of anger. She prayed that they wouldn't come true.

James held his head in his hands. It shook him to his very core to hear Dani suggest that Grace might not wake up. "Stop it. Stop! That is not going to happen. She'll wake up. She will."

The tension was icy thick in the waiting room. Voices passing by cut through the unbearable silence.

Lawrence whispered something in Dani's ear that had a calming effect on her. She nodded and he kissed her temple.

"Come on James, let's go," Lawrence said.

"What if she wakes up while I'm gone?"

Dani forcefully said, "She doesn't need you."

James had never really dealt with an angry Dani and it was frustrating. But he understood where it was coming from.

Lawrence lifted him up out of his chair. "It's okay. Let's go talk to the doctor and see if we can get an update. Dani will stay with Grace—she won't be alone."

James went into Grace's room and gazed at her. He gently squeezed Grace's hand and planted a kiss on her swollen forehead. He whispered in her ear that he loved her and he'd be back. He caught a glimpse of Dani glaring at him through the window before he reluctantly left with Lawrence.

After they were gone, Dani focused her attention to

Grace. Her heart seemed to hurt extra, in light of James' revelation. She didn't want to believe it, but she knew every word was true. Aside from disturbing, this news was devastating upon the already devastating news of Grace being in a coma. Dani was livid with both Grace and James, but she needed to sort through her feelings to see how to best handle everyone involved.

She slowly entered Grace's room and approached her bedside. She sat down and gently held Grace's hand. "Gracie—sweetie, you need to wake up. I need you... you're my best friend. Wake up so I can see your smiling brown eyes and hear your soothing voice. Wake up so we can laugh about all the funny things in life. Wake up so I can fuss at you for this. For scaring me half to death—about your accident... and... about James." Dani paused, contemplating her words. She sighed heavily before continuing.

"James, Gracie? You've been with James all this time? I don't understand how this could have happened. How could you let him do this to you? Why would you—oh, Gracie. Gracie."

Dani was at a loss for words for a moment. Holding Grace's hand, she continued. "You're going to be okay. Both you and the baby are going to be just fine. I'll take care of you until you're better. Just please wake up. Please, honey." Dani placed a kiss on the back of Grace's hand and rested it against her cheek.

Chapter 19

James and Lawrence were in the waiting room down the hall from Grace. There wasn't an update on her condition so, they were just talking and waiting.

"James..." Lawrence began. He could not remember the last time he had been this, to put it mildly, upset. "James, I don't even know where to begin in this entire mess."

"Well then, let me start for you. You're angry because—"

"I never took you for stupid," Lawrence jumped in. "But this entire situation reeks of it. Grace, James? Really? You set out a plan to seduce her? You must have been pretty convincing in order to get her to go along with this."

"Nylah... tried to be the voice of reason. She tried but my mind was already made up."

"Did you force her?" Lawrence almost choked on those words. Regardless of the situation, he knew force was not James' style—ever.

"Come on, man. Do you think I would force a woman? Do you think she would have let me handle her in such a way?"

"I would like to give Grace more credit than that.

However, I never expected her to let you handle her in this way, so I imagine anything could have been up for grabs. Why Grace?"

James reflected much about Lawrence's question. He had been reflecting on that for quite a while, actually. "Man, I don't know—it's crazy. My logic was all messed up. I wanted to be with someone... a secure relationship, but not within the confines of marriage—because of what happened with Janelle. I needed to be with someone who would be discreet, private—someone who would be good for me. Nylah was all of those things. She was also off limits, but I took great care to ignore that fact."

"Was it worth the risk—the consequence?"

"It's been tumultuous since she found out she was pregnant. She's felt the impact to a far greater magnitude than I have... this whole matter is my fault. Seeing her now, everything she has suffered because of me, none of this has been worth the risk... or the consequence. But it's too late. Whatever's going to happen now is going to happen. All I can do is pray for God's mercy." James felt his throat constricting. "They could have died—they have to be—be okay. She has to wake up. Lawrence, she has to."

Lawrence had never seen James like this before. Even when Janelle left him, he was many things, but among them Lawrence had sensed a little relief. Before him sat a broken man with nothing but pure, raw emotion: turmoil, anguish, hurt, sorrow; even an unveiling of a contrite heart. He could also see that, as wrong as this was, James did actually care about Grace.

"I didn't consider beyond what I wanted. God, very clearly, warned me about that. But I did nothing to stop the plan I had set in motion," James continued.

"What kind of warning did you receive?"

James clenched his jaw, inhaling and exhaling slowly. "I was told to either marry her, or leave her alone. I did neither—much to my regret. I should've married her, but I made it about me not wanting to get hurt again in that way. Never once considering how much I'd hurt her. I don't know how she's managed to put up with me for so long."

"You have not done well handling this, James."

"I know. I know. My dad said the same thing."

"Your parents—your parents know? How?" Lawrence was surprised.

"Once Nylah told my mother she was pregnant at your dinner table, Dad knew. He confronted me about it later. Nylah and I have both talked to my parents, separately and together. He gave me two weeks to handle it."

"Have you called them yet? About Grace? What about her family?"

James' eyes grew round. "I didn't even think to call my parents. I'll wait for an update first." James was momentarily quiet. "When I asked her about her family, all she said was that she had her reasons for not interacting with them. I didn't push her on it, especially since I had a lot of issues with Dad."

"Well, for what it's worth, I don't solely blame you. Maybe that's what shocks me most. Grace, of all people, allowed this to carry on for so long. And she never said anything to anyone."

"She's loyal—to a fault. And don't be fooled, she's strong willed—among other things."

Lawrence gave James a chastising glare. "Don't say anything else. It's too soon. I can deal with you, but Dani will need more time."

"I'm starting to see that."

"Listen, about the church—"

"I was actually on my way to talk to you about all of this when I got the call. I'm targeting next Wednesday to talk to the church. Of course, we need to meet with the board first, so I'll call an emergency meeting but I need to wait until Nylah wakes up."

"You'll step down temporarily and spend some time

getting yourself together. We'll let God handle everything else as He sees fit."

"Thanks, Lawrence. I appreciate you."

"Though you might right now, make no mistake about this: I am angry with you. I just realize being angry with you is not going to solve the situation."

James knew Lawrence would be upset for a while. But he was also grateful that he knew they would still have a friendship. That was something he needed in a serious way.

A nurse approached them and they stood hurriedly, anxious that she may have news about Grace.

"Mr. Garrison? We checked Ms. Anderson's stats and she seems to be stabilizing. She's still unconscious, but we expect her to come out of that, hopefully within the next 24 – 48 hours. The baby's heartbeat sounds strong. Everything appears to be all right and we'll do a full sonogram when she has stabilized more."

James breathed a deep sigh of relief at her news. *The baby sounds good.* He realized right then how much of a fool he had been. Grace was six months pregnant and he hadn't been to one appointment… hadn't heard the baby's heartbeat for himself. *What kind of man am I?* The answers to that question seemed like too many to face.

He and Lawrence returned to the waiting area. Lawrence poked his head into Grace's room to ask Dani to join him in the waiting room. When she finally joined them, Dani met James with a frosty glare.

"The nurse gave us an update," Lawrence said. He was trying to diffuse the tension between Dani and James.

Ignoring Lawrence, Dani's icy glare bore through James. "Why are you back—"

"Dani," Lawrence firmly warned. He checked her with an undeniable posture that told her this was not the time or the place to fight with James.

Dani bit down on her bottom lip in an attempt to appease her husband. She knew he was right. If she let Lawrence deal with James, as he had been, she wouldn't have to and that would be best for all involved. Not wanting Grace to be left alone for long, Dani listened to Lawrence's update and returned to Grace's room.

Lawrence shook his head as he glanced at Grace. He wanted to throttle both her and James. They had efficiently created a colossal mess with their relationship.

As the hours passed, they grew restless. Dani was still agitated with worry about Grace and just outright angry with James. Lawrence tried to make sure James and Dani didn't have need to cross paths, figuratively speaking. James was beside himself with everything. And they were all exhausted after an emotionally draining day.

Lawrence went to Dani close to one A.M., trying to persuade her to go home for a few hours. "I know you don't want to leave baby, but we won't be gone for long," he coaxed as she tried to protest.

"What if she wakes up and I'm not here?" Dani asked, leaning into Lawrence.

"Don't worry. James will call us as soon as anything happens."

Dani's countenance changed immediately upon the mention of James. She held her tongue but gave Lawrence an incinerating glare.

He met her gaze with one of his own. "That's another reason why we're leaving. Let's go. We'll be back in a few hours."

Dani begrudgingly complied. As they left, they turned back to James.

"We'll be back later. Call us if anything happens," Lawrence said.

"If she wakes up, tell her I'll be back. Make sure you tell her I was here, too." Dani's words were strained, as if it took enormous effort for her to be cordial.

James nodded at the both of them, finding words to be unnecessary. After they left, he sat at Grace's bedside and finally let the rest of his tears fall. One who rarely cried, he felt this was the only way to express how he felt. It crushed him to see her like this: so vulnerable, not able to move or talk.

More time passed, but still, no change with Grace. He held one of her hands and placed his other hand on her pregnant belly. He gently felt all around her belly, only the second time he had ever done so. As he moved across her, James was immediately alert. He promised he could feel the baby moving around inside. Could it be? This was all new to him. He leaned in closer to her, feeling a heightened awareness all around him.

"Hey. Hey, little baby. Are you there? It's me—it's your daddy." Those words seemed to jolt a shock through him. A few seconds later he felt a swift kick against his hand. Surprised by the sudden burst of activity, James decided to continue talking.

"I'm sorry I haven't been there for you. I'm sorry I haven't been there for your mom. I hope the both of you can forgive me and then I hope that we can be a real family." The baby kicked again as if agreeing with James.

"Your mom is sleeping right now, but I promise you, I'll take care of her. And we'll take care of you. Just do me a favor and help mommy wake up. Okay?" The baby kicked once more and James reached up to kiss Grace's belly in that same spot. He sat back down and put his head down praying that Grace would wake up soon. He almost didn't believe it... it was the slightest movement, but he felt her fingernails gently scratch across the palm of his hand.

He raised his head slowly, not sure if he imagined the movement he felt. Her hand moved again. James flew up beside her, stroking her face.

"Nylah? Nylah baby, I'm right here. I'm right here."

"James," she whispered.

"Sssshhh. You don't have to talk right now. Can you nod your head?"

Grace tried to nod, but James noticed her wince.

"Hurts," she whispered.

"Okay baby, you don't have to do that. You can squeeze my hand if you need to. Can you open your eyes?"

With a small amount of strength, Grace was able to blink her eyes open and she saw James standing right there next to her. She smiled at him and her eyes watered.

James felt his own tears rolling down from his eyes. He leaned forward to kiss her forehead. "Hey... welcome back."

Grace squeezed her eyes tight before opening them again. She cried her own tears as she felt an overwhelming sense of gratitude for being alive.

James pressed for the nurse to come to Grace's room. He would have run to get her, but he didn't want to leave Grace's side.

"Happened?" Grace struggled to ask. Her voice shifted from a whisper to a rasp.

James still didn't want her to do too much. "Shh, baby. We'll talk about that later."

Grace slightly shook her head no. "Please."

"Okay, okay. You were in a car accident. Do you remember anything?"

Grace thought for a moment. "A little."

James exhaled. *I'm not ready to hear these details.* "You don't have to tell me right now. I want you to get your strength back."

"S'okay. Talk-ing helps."

"Just not too much until after the doctor checks you out."

The nurse came in asking if everything was okay with Ms. Anderson. Seeing that Grace was awake, she smiled warmly and came over to check her vital signals.

"Ms. Anderson, I'm glad to see you back."

"The baby." Fear ran across her eyes and James tightened his hold on her hand to reassure her.

"So far, everything is fine. Dr. Hanks will give you a sonogram so you can see for yourself."

After the nurse left, Grace scanned James' face again. "Dani?"

"Lawrence and Dani were here earlier but left a few hours ago. I'm going to call and tell them you're awake."

A contemplative, worried, almost tearful concern glazed over Grace's face. "Emma?"

"Emma? What about Emma?" James was confused as to why Grace would ask about her.

"In car with—with me. She hurt?"

So Emma was the passenger they wouldn't mention by name. But what was she doing with Grace? James was well aware of the tension between Grace and Lisa. He was certain Lisa hadn't taken any of this well.

"No, baby. Emma wasn't hurt. They checked her out and released her to her parents."

"Good." Seeing James' inquiring eyes, Grace sought to temporarily appease him. "Long story. Later."

"Okay. Later."

"James?"

"Yes?"

"Thank you... being here. Love—love you."

James clenched his jaw, holding back every emotion that wanted to come out all at once. "I love you too, Nylah." He kissed her hand and wiped the tears from her eyes.

Grace closed her eyes, trying to rest some more. She was sore all over her body. The pain she felt made her anxious to hear the doctor's report. *As long as the baby is okay.*

"Are you in a lot of pain?" she heard James ask her.

She nodded even though it hurt. "All over."

James felt helpless, unable to do anything for her. "Do you want me to find the doctor?"

Grace felt a burst of panic arise in her. "Please don't... leave me. Stay... here—"

James heard the panic in her voice and did his best to soothe her. "I won't. I promise; I'll stay right here with you."

Grace calmed down a little and closed her eyes again,

trying to focus on making her breathing easier.

James momentarily stepped away from her bed to call Lawrence and tell him Grace was awake. He was observing her: she was trusting him right now. It had been a long time since she had trusted him at all. He could not let her down.

"Nylah. Lawrence and Dani will be here as soon as they can get here."

Grace opened her eyes slightly and whispered a little cheer. "Yay!"

They both turned at the sound of Dr. Hanks entering the room.

"Ah, Ms. Anderson!" he boomed. "So good of you to join us. Let's get you and this baby checked out." Turning to James, he said, "Sir, if you'll excuse us."

Grace immediately gripped James's hand as hard as she could. With the slightest shake of her head, she pleaded, "No. Nooo, he stays."

The doctor grinned as he addressed James. "Well, it seems Ms. Anderson's position is clear. You're free to stay if she desires."

"Don't worry, baby," he said to her. "I promised you I wasn't leaving you." James leaned down and whispered reassurances in her ear. She was fearful of something… he had to prove that he would be there with her and do what he could to protect her.

Grace calmed down again and slowly relaxed her grip on his arm. The nurse brought in the sonogram machine and set it up.

The doctor began Grace's check up, taking note of all the sensitive places where the most pain was. He asked her questions to check her cognizance and reflexes.

"All in all, you're going to be fine. You show no signs of brain trauma, but we'll run some more tests, just to be sure. You have considerable internal bruising and your body has had a traumatic experience. I'm placing you on bed rest for at least the next three weeks, to avoid any other stress on you and the baby. You are to involve yourself in no physical activity whatsoever, outside of general hygienic maintenance and eating."

"Now, let's take a gander at this baby." Dr. Hanks prepped Grace and placed the paddle on her abdomen. After a few seconds of swirling around, he found the baby. Then they heard the heartbeat, full and strong. The sound brought tears of relief to James and Grace's eyes.

"There's our baby," James whispered to Grace. She clasped her hand through his as they gazed at the monitor.

While they were viewing the baby, Dani and Lawrence had just arrived to the waiting area outside of Grace's room. Seeing how close they were upset Dani and she was about to charge into the room when Lawrence stopped her.

"Whoa! Hey... wait a minute," he said, pulling Dani back to him.

"What are you doing? I need to be in there with her."

"No. You need to really see them Dani," Lawrence motioned.

Through the window they saw James holding Grace's hand, talking to Dr. Hanks about the baby. They saw James kiss Grace's forehead and he said something to her that made her smile.

"Like it or not, she needs him right now. He's the one that needs to be in there with her. Yes, this is a mess. But we don't need to make it worse. We don't know how fragile Grace's condition is, and she needs all of us to do what we can, James included."

Dani's eyes watered in her continued frustration. She knew Lawrence was right, hard as it was for her to admit. She felt like she wanted to be mad at James forever, but that was not what Gracie needed from her.

"Fine. I'll behave. But—"

"No buts, Dani," Lawrence stated. "None."

They stayed outside in the hallway while Dr. Hanks continued with Grace.

"So, are you aware of the baby's gender?" Dr. Hanks asked.

"No," Grace answered. She had not wanted to find out without James. Now that he was here, maybe he wouldn't mind knowing.

"Do you want to know?"

Grace questioned James with her eyes.

"It's fine with me if it's fine with you," he answered her.

Grace turned back to Dr. Hanks. "Okay," she said with a slight nod.

"Well, congratulations folks. You'll be having a healthy baby boy in a few more months."

"A boy," they both gasped at the same time. James gave Grace a brief, intimate kiss on her lips. Looking into her eyes, he whispered, "Our boy."

Grace stroked the side of his face, embracing their bonding moment.

After Dr. Hanks left, Dani and Lawrence cautiously entered her room. James and Grace were discussing her condition and the baby and didn't hear them enter.

Dani lightly cleared her throat to get their attention. Grace, seeing her, immediately smiled and started to tear up. Dani rushed to the side of the bed and kissed her head.

"Gracie... I'm so glad you're okay. The baby is okay too, right?"

"Yes, the baby is fine," Grace slowly said. The more she talked, the easier it became. "Bed rest... internal bruising needs to heal, no added stress. Baby is just fine; no signs of distress. It's a boy!" Grace beamed at Dani and Lawrence.

"Y'all are having a boy?" Lawrence asked.

His use of the word 'y'all' did not escape Grace. Grace turned to James.

James confirmed her unspoken question with his answer. "I told them; they know everything."

Grace caught her breath. "Everything?" she whispered to James.

He nodded, stroking her hand in reassurance.

Grace examined Dani and Lawrence in light of this revelation. Friends who now knew the secrets she and James had held onto for so long. Grace felt the biggest sense of relief that the truth was finally out. Now it could be dealt with appropriately.

"Gracie can I talk to you alone?" Dani's voice was quiet but steady.

James jumped in, not wanting anything to upset Grace. "I told her I wasn't leaving her Dani, and she told you she doesn't need any added stress."

"James, I know how to interact with Grace," Dani said with considerable restraint. "I have no intentions of causing her any stress. I just want to talk to my friend without you in here. Is that all right? Please?"

Grace slipped her hand over James' hand, silently asking him to understand and give them some time alone.

"All right," he conceded to Grace. "I'll give you whatever you want. I'll be back in a little while." He kissed her forehead and headed for the door.

Eyeing Dani and Grace, Lawrence decided to get lost as well. "Uh, I'll go with James and leave you two alone. Grace, we'll talk later."

Dani gave her husband a grateful smile. He gave her one that said no stress for Grace and she nodded in compliance.

Lawrence followed James out. Grace smiled at the guys as they left, dimming out a little as she refocused on Dani.

"Gracie... I'm so glad you're back. I was so scared to lose you; the thought terrified me. Thank goodness Lawrence was with me because I would not have been able to handle any of this without him."

Grace was trying to find the right words to say to her friend. "You're not going to lose me. Who else is going to tell me when I'm wrong and love me anyway?"

"Gracie, I'll always love you." Dani took a pause before continuing, trying to focus her thoughts. She finally sighed.

"Why, Gracie? Why with James?"

"I don't know how it happened. It just did. And then, all of a sudden, we were being secretive."

Dani arched her eyebrows, but let Grace continue.

"Not all of it has been physical. We took time to know each other."

"Don't make this out to be some fairytale love story, Grace." Dani didn't mean to sound so chastising, but this was not a glamour story of love. It was more like truth and consequences. "At least he told us everything. I assume it was everything, anyway."

"What did he say?" Grace quietly asked.

Dani gave her the entire rundown of James' confession, complete with both her and Lawrence's reactions.

Grace internalized all that Dani had told her. James had completely surprised her... again. Maybe he—they were actually growing and making the right kind of progress this time. Evolving of sorts. James... James. Grace closed her eyes and rubbed her stomach. *Daddy loves us,* she thought. Just then, her body jolted at the feel of a swift kick.

"Gracie, are you okay?" Dani asked.

Grace opened her eyes to see her friend's face full of concern. She reached for Dani's hand and placed it on her stomach. The baby kicked again under Dani's hand and she smiled at the activity going on within Grace.

"I think somebody's glad to be alive," Dani mused.

Grace felt tears spring to her eyes.

Dani's eyes glazed over and a few spontaneous tears slid down her face. "We were really scared," she whispered. She wiped her face and put a little more strength into her voice. "You were unconscious and they told us you may have suffered a severe head injury. I was just scared and—"

"It's okay. I understand about being scared. Everything is fine. We're alive; Emma is fine. God is merciful."

"Yeah. About Emma—what was she doing with you?"

Grace gave Dani the edited version, careful not to break

Emma's confidence.

"How do you think Lisa responded?" Dani asked.

"I don't know. Hopefully, Emma was able to actually talk to her and Lisa listened to her."

"I guess only time will tell."

After a few quiet moments, Dani addressed another angle of this saga with Grace and James.

"Uh, Gracie, what exactly is the status of your relationship?"

"I think it's safe to say now that we're back together. I know he wants to be and we've definitely made strides on my part. I won't talk to him about it though, until he addresses the church. We probably never even really broke up, we just separated. I put the distance between us, and we held to it—for the most part."

"What does that mean? Wait. I don't think I want to know." Seeing Grace's face flush, Dani didn't know what to do. "No Gracie, please tell me y'all didn't!"

"I can't. Twice. I know, Dani. But it won't happen again. We promised."

"Promised who?" Dani skeptically asked.

"James' parents."

Dani's eyes grew double in size. "They know?" she whispered.

Grace nodded, feeling as if everything was finally coming full circle.

"You know what this means, don't you?" Dani asked her.

"I don't know if we're thinking the same thing."

"Valencia will blow her top!" Dani laughed.

Grace let out a surprised laugh. She hadn't been expecting Dani to say that, true as it was. "I told her she'd regret talking crazy to me," Grace recalled.

"Honey, she is going to have a FIT! Oh well, I guess it's for the best, concerning her. She was getting on my nerves, hounding James all the time," Dani said.

Grace shook her head, remembering that Valencia was the

one who asked James out.

Dani smiled. "It's good to hear you laugh."

"It's good to still have a friend to laugh with," Grace replied.

Dani reached to hug Grace. "I'm not going anywhere."

Chapter 20

James and Lawrence entered Grace's new private room out of the ICU, James freshly showered and changed with an overnight bag for Grace.

"Hey, lovely," he greeted, kissing Grace's forehead. "I picked up a few things for you... and someone who's here to see you."

Grace beamed with surprise when she spotted James' mother.

"Lady Garrison!" Grace exclaimed.

"Oh Grace, honey. How are you feeling?" she asked as she came to Grace's side.

"I'm sore and I want some real food. But, all things considered, I am well. Blessed to be alive, both the baby and I."

"I'm grateful to see and hear that you are well. I've been beside myself with concern; especially when James informed us of your condition. Now that I'm here, Dani and I will make sure you are completely taken care of."

Grace's heart swelled with love. "Thank you so much. Thank you."

"Oh, you're welcome, honey. We wouldn't have it any other way."

Later that afternoon, James and Katherine were talking in a corner, while Dani and Lawrence sat close by, keeping Grace company when Nathan appeared at the door. Grace was pleasantly surprised, but momentarily focused on James, whose face appeared set like stone. Grace then glanced at Lawrence.

Lawrence immediately understood. He went to go get James, who initially but quietly resisted.

Nathan was oblivious to that interaction since Dani distracted him with a greeting. While they were talking, Grace entreated with James again.

"Please," Grace mouthed to him. After a brief contemplation, James decided to go with Lawrence, but Grace could tell he was none too pleased to leave.

Turning to Nathan, Grace finally greeted him. "Hi Nathan," she said.

"Hey…" he returned, eyeing her cautiously. Sitting next to her bed, he paused before saying, "You know, if you needed attention, you could have just told somebody instead of scaring us half to death," he finished lightly.

Grace smiled back at him. "Well, you know, every now and then some of us like to make really big statements."

They bantered back and forth while Dani joined Katherine in the corner.

"What is with James?" Katherine murmured.

"He's jealous," Dani answered. "Grace and Nathan are really good friends and after he found out she was pregnant, he offered to take care of her and the baby—marry her—everything. It probably burns James up to see them still be able to interact so friendly."

"Ah, so he was competing for her affections?" Katherine asked.

"Not really. Grace has never been interested in Nathan beyond friendship. It's James that's making something out of nothing." Dani shrugged her shoulders nonchalantly. "He's just going to have to suck it up and accept the fact that they're friends. It will make things a lot easier."

Outside of Grace's room, Lawrence and James watched Grace and Nathan. James was seething from the inside out, intensified by the fact that Grace was the one who asked him to leave.

"She knows how I feel about Nathan. Why would she ask me to leave?"

Lawrence shook his head. "Man, you need to calm down. If you could see yourself, you would know exactly why. They're friends, James. They have been, way before you hooked up with her. He's checking on her after hearing she could have died; that's what friends do. You need to let it go because Grace doesn't need your unnecessary drama about it."

James instantly felt stupid. *Unnecessary drama... as in drama queen?* That sounded awful. Had he really been creating drama about it all this time? He needed to spend some major time in self-examination.

Back in the room, Nathan and Grace were laughing about a few reminiscent stories.

"Thanks again for coming, Nathan. I really appreciate it."

"Are you kidding me? I'm just glad you're okay. Because if something else would have happened, I don't think I—"

"Hey. Enough of that. We're good. We're okay."

"Listen Grace, about our last conversation, I just want to apologi—"

Grace held up her hand. "You don't have to apologize to me for anything. At all."

"I guess part of me felt like I pushed you away. And then another part was upset about the outcome of the situation. And then, we haven't exactly talked since then, so I didn't know where your head was or if you wanted to still be friends."

"I actually feel that I owe you an apology."

"Hey... forget about it," Nathan said.

"Are you okay with us just being friends?" Grace asked him.

Nathan nodded. "I'm good with just being friends. If I would have listened when you tried to tell me before, that friends are all we've ever been or will be, we could have avoided a really awkward situation."

Grace let out a relieved sigh. After their conversation ended, Nathan said his goodbyes and left.

James and Lawrence came in a few moments later. James was brooding again.

"James, come here please," Grace beckoned.

He came over and sat next to her bed. "Yes?" he asked.

"What's the matter?" Grace asked.

"I'm an idiot," James answered.

Caught off guard by his answer, Grace let out a surprised laugh.

"It's not much fun realizing how much of a jerk you've been for so long," he finished.

Grace reached out to stroke the side of his face. "Well, we're all grateful for your progress."

James grunted and tried to hide his amusement.

"I asked you to leave because—"

"You don't have to explain."

"So, are we good?" Grace asked.

James kissed her palm. "We're definitely good."

Dr. Hanks came in right then, prepared to give them an update and a few mandates.

James sat on one side of Grace, Dani and Katherine sat on the other, Lawrence standing behind them.

"Well, Miss Anderson, it seems that you will be able to go home in a couple of days. We need to keep you for observation, but you'll be free to go on Friday." Turning to the others, he said, "We need to make sure you all understand her condition.

"I'm not sure where you'll be staying, but stairs are out of the question. No physical activity, especially the next few weeks. Maybe after one or two week's time, you can do very light movement around your residence, but not for long. Until then, nothing. And definitely not anything else for at least three weeks. That includes any kind of se—"

"We understand," Grace said, cutting him off. She felt a deep, embarrassing blush settle in her cheeks.

"Okay," Dr. Hanks smiled. "No large crowds, and you don't need to go out anywhere except the clinic for your weekly check-up. Absolutely no stress," he warned everybody.

"If you can sleep on a soft but firm mattress, that will be best."

"We'll take care of it," James said.

Dr. Hanks gave them a few more instructions concerning Grace's care and said he would be back tomorrow to check on her and left.

The group discussed the best options for Grace's care.

"Lawrence, Gracie can stay with us, right?" Dani asked him.

"No!" Grace responded.

"Nonsense, Gracie. We need to take care of you. You can't go back to your apartment. James, tell her," Dani implored.

"Oh, now you want James' help," Grace sarcastically stated.

"Dani, wait," James said. "Nylah, please don't get worked up; you know we all have to decide what's the best option for you. Okay?"

"Are you trying to patronize me?" Grace asked him. He was holding her hand and stroking her fingers, effectively accomplishing the task of relaxing her.

"Not at all," James smiled. "But you're going to have to let us take care of you."

Grace sighed, but didn't argue with him. "Okay," she said, motioning for them to proceed.

"Okay, so you can stay with us," Dani said.

"Dani, I sincerely appreciate the offer, but I would feel really uncomfortable staying in your house."

"If you don't stay with us, where will you go?" Dani asked.

"Nylah can stay at my house," James offered.

"James, don't even think—" Dani started.

"Wait a minute. Before you give me the run-down, let me explain. Dani, as you stated, Nylah cannot go back to her apartment." Turning to Grace, James said, "You know you can't go there."

"Why not? We have elevators."

"What if something happens to them? Then it's three flights of stairs up and down. It's not the best or the safest option for you. Additionally, by your own words, you don't feel comfortable staying with Dani and Lawrence. My house is the best option for you."

Feeling a little more persuasion was needed, James went ahead. "It's a level one story, with plenty of space. Mom will already be there with you and Dani will have access to come and go. If you don't go to my house, then the only other possible option is a hotel and that's just illogical. Besides, you're comfortable at my house."

The rest rolled their eyes at his last statement.

"Not helping," Grace said in a sing-song voice.

"Sorry, but it's true."

"You seem to be forgetting something, James," Dani voiced. "You happen to live at your house. So what about you?"

"I can go to a hotel. That's easy." James paused, waiting for a response. "Is there a better solution?"

Lawrence spoke up. "Grace, James brings up several well-made points. The decision is not without your input. What do you decide?"

Grace was slightly overwhelmed at their rally to help her. "Okay. I'll stay at James' house."

They let out a sigh of relief.

"Thank you," James said, kissing her on her forehead. "All right, we'll make sure everything is ready by Friday, so until then, there may only be one of us with you at a time. We'll take shifts to make sure you're not alone. Is that okay?"

Grace nodded, realizing she was glad she didn't have to worry about anything.

"Thank you all," Grace told them.

During the course of the evening and the next day, they were busy working to make sure Grace had everything she needed. Dani and Katherine took turns staying with her at the hospital, while James and Lawrence and whichever one of the ladies was not on shift, took care of everything around the house.

Thursday afternoon, Dani and Grace were talking when there was a knock on the door.

"Come in," Grace called out.

Lisa came in, Emma right behind her. Grace's eyes watered seeing them. Emma rushed to Grace's bed.

"Grace, are you okay? I've been praying for you and the baby, trying not to worry. I'm so sorry; this is all my fault. You never would have been out there if it weren't for me. Please, forgive me," Emma said, starting to cry.

Grace thought her heart would break. She could not allow Emma to carry guilt over this. "Emma."

Emma lifted her red eyes to Grace.

"Honey, this is not your fault. You had no control over what happened; it was an accident. Your prayers helped me, I'm sure, so thank you for that. Praying for me and the baby was the right thing to do. We're fine, thank God."

"Are you sure you're okay? You're not just saying that to make me feel better?"

Grace held up her right hand. "You can even ask the nurses if it makes you feel better."

Emma smiled brightly and covered Grace's hand with her hand.

Lisa finally spoke up. "Hi, Grace. Hi, Dani." She sounded hesitant but stepped forward, cautiously.

"Hi, Lisa," they replied.

Grace motioned to her, trying to make her feel more comfortable. "You can sit down if you'd like."

"Are you sure?"

"Yes. Emma, you can sit on my bed. It's okay, you won't hurt me."

After they were settled, Dani moved to a quiet corner of the room, but listened to make sure Grace didn't become stressed.

Lisa went first. "When the hospital called me, I went ballistic—crazy, upset, hurt, everything. I called my husband and he had to check me in the car, on our way to pick up Emma. I've been so self-centered for months... Anyways, he told me I needed to start thinking about the reasons Emma would call you, and not us.

"When we got home, Emma told us what happened and what you said to her." Lisa's eyes watered. "Even after the way I've treated you, you still defended me to her. Grace, I am so sorry. We were supposed to be friends and I've said some hurtful things about you. And to say them to Emma, that's just—" Lisa's voice broke.

"When Emma told us that you turned the car so she wouldn't get hit, I completely broke down. You risked your life and your baby's life to save my daughter's life. Words will never be enough to express our gratitude to you. We've talked to her about the situation, her actions and her resulting consequences. But we are very grateful there was somebody she could trust that would try to tell her the right things."

"Thank you for that," Grace said.

"We're so glad you're well."

Lisa and Grace talked for a while about the past year. They laughed and cried, addressing the positives and negatives of their friendship. Lisa even acknowledged that Grace had a positive influence on Emma, and Lisa thanked her for that.

Lisa expressed the hurt and disappointment she felt when she found out Grace was pregnant, but told her she had come to understand that it was her own experiences and the reflection those instances had upon herself that contributed to her overall reaction.

"It was really hard for me to face that, but talking to Emma helped me tremendously," Lisa said.

Emma smiled at her mother and at Grace.

"Are you in a lot of trouble?" Grace asked Emma.

Emma nodded. "Yes, and for a long time. But it's for my good… and I rather it be this than something else."

"Well, all we can do is learn," Grace said. "If we strive for positive growth, we'll all be better for it."

After time, Lisa and Emma said their goodbyes. "When you're settled, we'll check in on you, okay? Right, Mom?" Emma asked.

"Yes honey, we will. Let's go now, so Grace can rest more."

"Yes, ma'am. Love you, Grace!"

"Love you too, honey."

After they left, Dani came back over beside Grace. "You okay?"

Grace nodded. "Yeah, I'm good. It's getting late. Why don't you go home?"

"And feel the wrath of James for leaving you alone? Absolutely not," Dani smiled.

Grace smiled back, but it was strained. "Um, wher-where is James? I mean, I guess he's at the house right?"

"Yeah. He's been trying not to micro-manage everybody, but you know how he gets."

Grace was really quiet, not responding to Dani's statement.

"Gracie… are you sure you're okay?"

"Yeah, I'm just tired. Really, you can go home. Or over to the house to make sure everything is okay."

"Do you really want me to leave?" Dani asked her.

"I'm just going to go to sleep. I'll be fine. You all need rest just as much as I do."

Dani was a bit skeptical, but decided to leave. She knew then what Grace needed, even though Grace wouldn't tell her.

"Okay, honey. I'll see you tomorrow, okay?"

"Thanks Dani."

After Dani left, Grace felt the tears roll down. She knew she was feeling cranky and overly sensitive, but she hadn't seen or talked to James since yesterday. She hadn't expected it to affect her so strongly, though. *Ugh… get it together, Grace.* She tried to go to sleep, but her emotions made her a little restless. She turned on the TV and came across a good show, helping to distract her some… but not much.

****

Lena was at Michelle's house having dinner with the family. Edward was there too, talking to Michelle's husband, Rand in the other room. Her daughters were getting ready for bed and Lena and Michelle were catching up like they usually did throughout the week.

Michelle hushed her voice and leaned forward to speak to Lena secretively. "I didn't tell you about James, did I?" she asked.

Lena shook her head, but she felt her heart beat intensify.

"Remember when you asked me about him? Well, we found out that his girlfriend is pregnant. As if that wasn't bad enough, she's in the hospital right now from being in a bad car accident. That's why Mom's not here. She went to see about them."

"Oh, my gosh! Well, is she okay? Have you heard anything else?" Lena was genuinely surprised to hear that Grace was in the hospital. She hadn't talked to James in about a week.

"Mom said she woke up from her coma, thank God. She should be out of the hospital tomorrow and Mom's going to stay for a while to help take care of her." Michelle shook her head. "James... I don't even know what to say about him right now."

"Wow. This is crazy. What about your dad? He could not have been happy about this."

"You already know. Dad was livid. He's leaving on Monday to go be with them, and to help concerning the church."

Lena exhaled but decided not to say anything else. She didn't want to let on that she had been in contact with James and already knew about Grace's pregnancy. She observed Michelle staring at her.

"What is it? Why are you staring at me?" Lena asked. *Please don't let her know.*

"You're keeping something from me," Michelle stated.

Oh God, no. "Really? You think so? Well, what is it then?" Lena asked as nonchalantly as possible. She held her breath in waiting.

"Who is Harrison Carter?" Michelle asked.

Lena let out a slow, relieved breath. *Oh, good. I can do this.* "I wish I knew. Do you know him?"

"No. But I saw him staring at you and I asked around until someone told me his name. Are you seeing him?"

"Not at all. I have no desire to see him and I've told him so."

"You've talked to him? How come you didn't tell me?"

Lena chuckled. "He contacted me. I'm surprised you're excited about this."

"Only because you've actually talked to him. Though, I would prefer if you didn't talk to *him*. There's something about him that I don't trust," Michelle stated.

"Well, you don't have anything to worry about. I do not intend on talking to him again."

Michelle shrugged. "Sometimes men are persistent. Just be

careful."

"Always." *I guess I'm safe.*

"But since we're talking about men…" Michelle smiled.

Lena groaned. *I guess I'm not safe after all.*

****

"James," Dani called out. She had just arrived at his house.

"We're back here, Dani," he called back.

Dani went to where Grace's room was setup, to find her husband, Katherine and James.

"Hey," Lawrence said, going to greet her. "How's Grace?" he asked her.

"She's… okay," Dani answered carefully.

James had appeared inattentive, until Dani had given her answer. Staring intently at her, he asked, "Wait. If you're here, then who's with Nylah?"

"Nobody. She suggested that I go home to rest."

"Dani, you weren't supposed to leave her—"

Dani stopped him. "James." Pausing, she thought about her next words. "She doesn't need me right now. She asked where you were, but wouldn't open up. As her friend, if I know for certain that she needs something, I'll try my best to do it. Despite our differences right now, I recognize more and more the impact your presence has had on her. She hasn't seen you since yesterday; she needs to see you. She needs to talk to *you*."

Digesting Dani's words, he was struck speechless, his mind racing.

Breaking his thoughts, his mom said, "James, we can handle this. Go. Now."

Without another word, James left, leaving them to finish setting the house up for Grace.

****

James opened Grace's hospital room door softly, trying to be quiet in case she was sleep. He closed it carefully and took a few steps into the quiet room. She was turned on her side, her back facing him. He thought she was actually sleep, but then he heard a sniffle. He stopped for a few moments, not sure if he heard right. Then he heard it again. *Is she crying? Did something happen?*

Feeling his heart beat faster in his chest, he cautiously approached her. "Nylah," he called out softly.

"James?"

"Yeah, baby. It's me."

Grace stayed on her side, but extended her hand, beckoning him to come to her.

He took her hand and sat, facing her. "Nylah, what's wrong? Did something happen?"

She shook her head. "No. Nothing happened."

Wiping her tears, he asked, "Then why are you crying?"

Sniffling again, she said, "Because I missed you. I think I'm being a little overly sensitive. I just got really sad when I realized I hadn't seen or talked to you in a full 24 hours. It's silly…"

"Hey, no it's not; I should have at least called you. I'm sorry, baby," James said, kissing her hands.

"You don't have to apologize. I know you were at the house. Is everything finished?"

"I left my mom, Dani and Lawrence there. I'm sure they've got it under control."

"Dani said you were trying not to micro-manage," she teased, bringing a chuckle out of both of them.

"Yeah, I don't think I've been real successful with that. They were probably ready for me to leave. Speaking of leaving, why are you sending away people that are supposed to be here with you?"

"I know you wanted someone to be here. But some alone time was good for me."

"Maybe she's not the one you wanted… or needed?" James inquired.

"Yes," Grace answered after a pause. "Your company was all I wanted right now."

"I got so caught up in fixing your room, it hadn't dawned on me that I was neglecting you."

"You were pre-occupied. I understand," Grace assured James.

"Maybe too much. I've been too pre-occupied. And you've been far more than understanding with me. Too understanding, too forgiving…"

"Stop. Please. We've both made a lot of wrong choices. Can we just choose to do what's right from now on? Can we find a way to make it right… to make us work?"

"Is that what you want? To make us work?"

"Yes. That's what I want." Grace smiled at James.

After a few silent moments, James asked, "Are you otherwise feeling okay?"

"Yeah. You're not going to leave are you?"

"No—no, baby. I'm not going to leave until they release you tomorrow and I can take you home."

"Home…" Grace repeated, reaching up to stroke his face.

Kissing her palm, he gazed intently at her. "Yeah. Home. If I have my way, you'll never leave once we get there."

"James," Grace hesitantly started, "when are y—"

"Wednesday," he answered.

Grace's eyes grew in size. "Really?"

"Yes. It's past time. But we can talk about it after you get out of here. Is that all right?"

Grace nodded. Feeling a total relaxation replace her restlessness, she yawned and sighed heavily.

"Go to sleep now. Don't worry; I'll be here."

Grace tugged at him. James stood over her and leaned down to give her a kiss. "Goodnight, baby."

"When you get tired, you can sleep next to me," she said, repositioning her body.

"Okay." James stroked her scalp until she had drifted off, sound asleep. Then he sat back in his chair and watched her, his mind going back over their conversation.

I missed you... Can we just do what's right from now on? Can we find a way to make it right... to make us work? That's what I really want.

She really wanted to be with him. She was ready for them to try again, finally. That realization settled deep within him.

He was going to talk to the church on Wednesday. That was going to be extremely difficult... nonetheless, it would be done. And then, he was going to marry Grace. If she agreed, they would be married soon. It couldn't be soon enough for him.

James noted that she appeared a bit more peaceful as she slept. He felt profound regret about screwing up her life for the past year. He wished he could take it all back, starting with his motives. She had deserved better than what he had offered her.

Shaking his head in disgust, he felt, for the first time, an explosive anger directed at himself. He really needed help—God's help.

As time passed, he felt his eyes closing, sleep taking over him. *When you get tired, you can sleep next to me...* James wondered if it were a bad idea. Deciding that there was no ill intent in her suggestion or his thoughts to do so, he carefully situated himself next to her on the bed, atop the covers. She must have subconsciously adjusted, tucking herself against his side. He placed his arm around her and drifted off to sleep.

****

James woke up at the buzz of his phone in his pocket. Yawning, he saw that it was his mother calling.

"Hello," he answered quietly.

"James, are you both all right? Did I wake you?" Katherine asked.

"Yes, and yes. We're fine and sleep."

"How is Grace?"

"She's all right. She's been sleep almost all night."

"Oh, good. How was she when you arrived last night?"

"Emotional. And yes, she did want me here with her." Glancing at Grace he added, "I'm glad I came. Is everything ready?"

"Yes, son. Everything is ready. We'll see you when you get here."

They hung up and James bent down to kiss Grace's forehead. She stirred, but didn't wake up.

"I can't wait to marry you," James whispered. "The day you become my wife will be one of the happiest days of my life. Thank you for putting up with me. I promise—and I sincerely mean promise—to take care of you and our baby, to love you, to honor you, and to cherish you forever."

James watched her sleep until she finally woke up. He helped her get ready, and after all of Grace's paperwork was taken care of, James helped her into a wheelchair and took her downstairs. The nurse waited with her while James went to get his car. He pulled around and carefully helped her into the car.

Grace was quiet at first, but in a few minutes time she and James had engaged themselves in an amusing conversation on the way to James' house. It was light enough to keep Grace from getting excited and entertaining enough to keep her attention. Before she knew it, they were pulling up to James' house.

"I'll be right back," James said. He got out and entered the house. He was back within a few moments.

"Are you ready?" he asked Grace.

"Yeeees. Please take me inside."

Reaching for her, she looped her arms around his neck and he carefully extracted her from the car. Grace laid her head on his shoulder and sighed.

"You are so spoiled," James teased, carrying her through the open entrance.

Grace smiled at his statement. "You have indeed spoiled me quite well," she remarked with a glint in her eyes.

"I'm not done spoiling you yet. Not by a long shot."

"Promise?" Grace asked.

"Forever," James answered, placing a kiss on her temple.

"*Gracie!*" Dani squealed, running up to them. "I'm so glad you're out. Now, you don't have to worry about anything; we've got it all under control. Your room is over here. This way, James."

"Dani, this is my house. I know which way to go."

"She's just excited," Grace told James. "She's probably also trying to keep herself from thinking about the fact that I also know exactly where we're going."

That verbal reminder about how much time Grace had spent at his house brought memories upon James. He had really missed her. The entire situation made him feel melancholy.

Grace noticed the change in his demeanor but decided to wait until later to remark upon it. She let him carry her to her room in silence. Well, not complete silence. Dani was chatting about something, but Grace wasn't paying attention to her.

They reached the room and James settled her on the bed and helped her get comfortable. Dani sat at the foot of her bed while James left to get her belongings. He returned, but prepared to leave again. Grace was hoping he would stay for a while.

Grabbing his hand, she momentarily stopped him. "I wanted to talk to you," she quietly relayed.

"I'll be back a little later. Let Dani stay with you, or get some rest."

Grace knew her facial expression showed her disappointment, but she couldn't help it. "How long will you be gone?" she whispered.

"I'll be back when you wake up."

She didn't know why, but she was dismayed at the prospect of his absence and it showed on her face.

James kissed against her hair. "I promise I'll be back. I love you."

"James…" Grace whimpered. She was losing her composure, the more she tried to keep it.

He squeezed her hand and left.

Grace closed her eyes, feeling the tears stinging inside them. She fought them as hard as she could. Opening her eyes, she found Dani staring at her. Grace had momentarily forgotten Dani was sitting on her bed. She thought Dani was going to chastise her for acting so clingy with James.

Instead, Dani wanted to comfort Grace. Observing Grace and James up close and personal was a telling experience. Their bond went beyond fondness. At first, Dani wasn't so sure because of the nature of their relationship. She had found it hard to believe, once the truth came out, that James could be less than selfish, self-serving and shallow. He was slowly proving her wrong. Dani wasn't sure why he'd left so quickly, but she could see that it pained him to go as much as it pained Grace to see him go.

Going around the bed to sit next to Grace, Dani hugged her gently. "It's okay, Gracie; you can cry if you want to."

Grace shook her head in frustration. "I don't know what's wrong with me. I act like I can't be away from him for two seconds without having a fit."

"You've been through a lot. I think the both of you—maybe all of us—are realizing how important you two are to each other. Besides, you also have to contend with your emotions and hormones. I think that comes with the territory of being pregnant."

"I feel so ridiculous sometimes; like I need to be stronger than this, like I'm being too weak."

"You're not used to letting people help you. I'm surprised you've let us help you this much."

"I don't have a choice."

"Well, maybe that's good for you Gracie. Maybe you need to be in a position where you can't do anything. Only heal, only do what's best for you and the baby."

Grace sensed a double meaning to some of Dani's words. She knew she would do well to take to heart and heed to them.

Dani cleared her throat and held up a book.

Grace let out a laugh. "You're going to read *The Berenstain Bears* to me?"

"Yes, yes I am," Dani grinned. "I'm going to read to you and you're going to go back to sleep. You're not going to worry about anything except having pleasant dreams and sleeping well."

"You're right." Reaching for Dani's hand, Grace gave it a light squeeze. "Thanks," she told her.

"Of course, honey. Anytime. Now just relax…"

Grace settled into the bed and was prepared to listen for at least a few pages. As Dani read the title, Grace closed her eyes. By page three, she was sound asleep. Dani closed the book, and made sure Grace at least appeared comfortable. She turned out the light and pulled the door almost closed knowing she would check on her periodically.

Dani was talking to Katherine when James and Lawrence came back to the house a few hours later. James immediately went to Grace's room to check on her before joining the rest of them in the family room.

While they were chatting, James got up and went to Grace's room. He opened the door to find her wide awake. Smiling, he went inside.

"Hey. You're up. How do you feel?" James sat down beside her bed.

"Better rested." Grace motioned for him to prop extra pillows up behind her and help her sit up.

"Do you need anything?"

"I'm so hungry," Grace said.

"Okay. I'll rectify that right now. I'll be back in a few minutes."

James came back in about two minutes, empty handed.

"What happened?" Grace asked.

"Mom and Dani will bring your food."

Grace smiled at him, amused. "You're not going to run away from me again are you?"

James gave her an apologetic grin as he sat down. "No. Sorry about that. I just needed to clear my head and let you rest."

"Anything you want to talk about?" Grace asked, reaching for his hand.

James paused. "Yes. Are you sure you're up for a conversation?"

Grace nodded her head.

James pulled his chair as close to Grace's bed as possible and took her hand. "Nylah, I want to marry you. Will you marry me?"

"After you talk to the church?" Grace asked.

James nodded.

Grace's eyes softened into a loving gaze. "James... are you sure?"

James' eyes glistened. "Yes. I know that I left you. I abandoned you... I deserted you... there's no excuse for that. I never should have let you go away from me and I am so sorry. I understand if you don't want to marry me, but I'm asking you because I love you. Just like when I asked you before. That's never changed. And I would be so happy and so grateful if you—"

Grace placed her hand over James' mouth and lightly ran her fingers across his lips. "You know that I love you," Grace softly began. "And despite my consistent frustration with you over the past few months, my desire to marry you has never changed. Where's my ring?"

James pulled it out of his pocket and placed it on her finger. He sighed gratefully, kissed her hand and smiled at her. "I love you," he whispered.

"Love you, too," Grace responded.

There was a slight knock on the door before Dani and Katherine entered with food for Grace. They observed James and Grace and the ring on her finger.

Katherine came around and sat next to Grace. "Soooo… there's a huge ring on your finger that wasn't there earlier. Any news?"

"Yes, ma'am. James and I are getting married."

Katherine wrapped her arm around Grace. "That's great, honey. That's great."

"We heard you were hungry, so we brought you a tray," Dani said.

Grace observed the delightful tray of food: a grilled cheese BLT, pickle slices, and a cup of fruit. They also brought her some sweet water, which was water infused with strawberries and mint, and mildly sweetened with honey. She clapped her hands in cheer. "Real food excites me right now," she laughed.

Lawrence came in and they all sat around talking while she ate.

"Dad will be here on Monday," James told Grace. "He and Lawrence are going to oversee church operations while I'm out." Pausing, he regarded Grace. "I'm also going to ask him if he'll marry us."

"Really?" the others said in unison.

"Are you sure?" Lawrence asked.

"Yes. What do you think, Mom? Do you think he'll do it?"

"I think your father would say yes. You know he'll talk to the both of you beforehand. Since you plan to marry soon, you need to devote at least three days prior to pre-marital counseling, and plan for extended post-marital counseling. Your father and I will do one session," Katherine said.

"Dani and I will do one session," Lawrence chimed in.

"And we'll ask Elder and Sister Rollins to do the last," Katherine finished.

"When do you plan to marry?" Dani asked them.

"I haven't discussed this with Nylah yet, but I was hoping for next Sunday." James was gazing intently at Nylah, trying to gauge her reaction. She seemed unfazed.

Grace said, "The sooner the better." Cautious about her next question, she turned to Dani and Lawrence. "We know that you are very disappointed and upset with us; rightfully so. But you two are our closest friends. Would you consider standing up for us during the ceremony?"

Through an unspoken exchange, Dani and Lawrence made a decision. "Of course we'll stand up for you Gracie," Dani said. "If anything, Lawrence and I are definitely going to make sure that you two do get married."

Relieved, Grace expressed her thanks. "You two are the best. Thank you."

"James, when is your meeting?" Grace asked him.

"Most of us met today—it was more impromptu, so they only know I'll be stepping down, but they don't know why."

"I'm going to church on Wednesday," Grace said.

Everyone replied simultaneously with their objection.

"No," James replied.

"No, ma'am," Dani stated.

"That's not a good idea Grace," Lawrence said.

"Honey, don't do that," Katherine admonished.

Grace shook her head. "It doesn't matter what you say."

"Grace," Katherine began, "the doctor warned you about your activities. You have strict orders not to go anywhere; you need to follow them—for you and the baby."

Grace knew she was right, but she was determined not to be swayed. "I won't do anything or go anywhere else. But I am going to be there."

"No, you're not," James firmly stated. "This is not up for discussion."

Grace stared at him. He had never taken such a strong stance with her before. Sure he had been firm or insistent, but not like this. She was trying to figure out how to respond to him when the others dismissed themselves.

"Well, that's our cue to leave you two to this discussion. We'll be in the family room," Katherine said. They all got up and left, leaving James and Grace to talk.

"James, I—"

"Nylah, why are you even trying to go?" James was about three paces from fury at her insistence.

Grace's eyes watered as she contemplated her answer. She wasn't sure how he would take it, but she decided to be as honest as she could about it.

"Because I remember what it felt like when I had to go through it and I only knew of one person who would be there for me. And I just want to be there for you..." Grace twisted her hands, trying to blink away her tears. She didn't want to make James feel bad for not being there for her and after a few minutes of silence, she lifted her head to see genuine remorse on his face.

"I'm so sorry," James whispered. Wiping his eyes, he continued. "That instance plays in my head all the time. I'll never forget any detail of it, especially the fact that I'm the one who put you there."

"I'm not trying to make you feel bad, James."

James sat next to her on the bed. He wrapped his arm around her and grabbed her hand. "Your willingness to support me is both mind-blowing and overwhelming. You've already given me so much that I don't deserve. But I can't let you go to the church. No objections."

Grace leaned against him and cried. "I don't want you to be alone."

James hated for Grace to cry. It crushed him every time. "Nylah... baby... I can't." *I think this is the first time I have ever actually told her no.* "It would be really irresponsible to let you go, and I've been far too irresponsible long enough. Please promise you won't try to go against my wishes."

"I don't want to promise you that," Grace tearfully said.

"Nylah, I'm asking you to promise me to stay here. Promise me."

Grace relented, knowing she wouldn't win this battle.

"Fine. I promise I won't go. Will you come here after service?"

"There is no way I wouldn't come see you, especially after that." Holding Grace's hand he added, "Thank you."

"For what?" Grace sniffed.

"For teaching me how to love someone unconditionally... sacrificially. I admire you for how you've handled yourself in this situation, having to deal with me. There are so many different ways this could have gone, but you always tried to consider the big picture instead of the selfish picture. I have been a fool."

"I'm having a baby. I can't afford to be selfish in a foolish way."

"Not everyone thinks that way. Suffice it to say, you're a remarkable woman."

"James," Grace started after a few quiet moments, "Do you ever wonder what our relationship would be like if we had done it the right way?"

"All the time. God warned me to either stay away from you or marry you early on. I felt like I couldn't do either one, which I am so sorry for. I'm certain our relationship would be very blessed, instead of wrapped in turmoil."

When Grace fell quiet again, James sensed he should give her some time to rest.

James kissed her hand. "I should go. I'll be back tomorrow. I love you."

"I love you, too. Goodnight."

****

James sat alone in his car, needing to have a talk with God.

"God."

James.

"God, I'm sorry." James was feeling the weight in stages, and it was increasingly overwhelming. "Will Nylah and the baby be okay? What about the church? Me? Will I ever be okay?"

They will be fine. The church will need much healing time, but if they seek Me for help, they will be fine too. You need to spend time with Me if you desire full deliverance, healing, and restoration. Your sins are forgiven, but you need to be made whole.

James talked with God all night, praying that all was not lost for him.

Chapter 21

James sat on the front row next to his father. He had cleaned out his office Monday after his meeting with the board. That meeting had not gone well, as there was a hefty amount of anger expressed regarding James' relationship with Grace. The board did agree to allow Lawrence to take over as pastor, once they were sure he and Dani had no knowledge of the true nature of James and Grace's relationship.

James sat now, feeling that this was indeed the hardest thing he has ever had to do. That weight rested on him in a remarkably heavy way. He watched while Lawrence stood in the pulpit, in front of the congregation and told the church that he had stepped down as pastor, effective Monday after a meeting with the church board.

James heard the frenzy of voices and even someone from the back let out a surprised, "*What?*"

Lawrence motioned for him to come speak and right before he got up, his father gave him a pat on the back. James didn't know why, but that seemed to give him strength.

James approached Lawrence, feeling every emotion possible. Turning to face the people, James cleared his throat and examined the many faces of people who had trusted him as their leader.

"Over the past few years," he started, "I've been preaching to you about righteousness and sinful natures, but I have not been living according to those biblical standards. I don't deserve your respect in my position as a pastor because I, myself, have not respected the position."

He could hear the muffle of murmurs from people who wondered where this was headed.

"Eleven months ago, I pursued an intentionally inappropriate relationship. Since April of this year, that intent and desire became the reality." James paused to clear his throat again, feeling some tears begin to cloud his vision. "I have been involved with Nylah Anderson... Grace Anderson," he heard an audible shock in the congregation, "and our relationship resulted in her current pregnancy. The child she carries is mine."

There was dead silence, but to James it was one of the most deafening sounds ever. *This is me right now. My time has come.* At that moment, James didn't know what had happened. He felt his body bend over and he began to weep.

"I am so sorry," he heard himself say, not knowing if he was talking to God or to the people before him. He felt things internally that he had never allowed himself to feel before: guilt, shame, a desire for true repentance and help from God.

He felt the presence of someone near him and after he collected himself to continue, he straightened up to find Lawrence standing on one side of him and his father on the other.

Seeing the devastation on the faces of the members almost undid him again, but he knew he needed to get through this.

"I have not been right for a long time," he rasped. "I ignored a lot of things in me that has enabled me to stand before you today. I never considered the reproach I was bringing upon God, but I can tell you that at this very moment, I am truly sorry for it. I apologize to you for putting the church in this position. I'm sorry for perpetuating a life that does not agree with God's standards.

"I am a selfish and irresponsible person, and those are two traits that I refused to face about myself. I can't hide any longer."

James paused and thought about some things he needed to clarify. "Lawrence and Dani had no idea about my relationship with Nylah. They were just as shocked, if not more so, than you are. It was our secret because that's what we decided we wanted.

"Our relationship was mutual, but it was my idea. Our sin is great and my heart is heavy. I know she stood before you a few months ago, and I also apologize that I allowed that to happen without voicing my involvement in the matter."

James' tears had never stopped falling, but he had been able to keep from totally breaking down again. He surveyed faces across the church and processed the different emotions he saw: anger, hurt, disappointment, bewilderment. *These people may never want to talk to me again.*

"There is no excuse for what I've done and I understand that any mess or fallout from this is on me. I've entreated God for mercy and all I can do now is let go, fully give myself over to God and let Him fix what is broken inside of me. I met with the church board and have stepped down as pastor. Lawrence will operate in the pastoral position, with my father overseeing some operational issues as well. I have a serious period of restoration that I need to go through and after that, all I can do is see what God says.

"In the meantime, Nylah and I intend to marry soon. I know that many of you are upset and beyond. What you feel is certainly justified. All I ask is that if you can find it within you to pray for us, please do so. We stand in great need of your prayers."

Wiping his face, James didn't know if there was really anything else he could say.

He went back to his seat and just stared at the floor. In

the background he heard Lawrence admonish others against involving themselves in ungodly manners of conversation and that if anyone had something to say or ask, they could come to him.

After benediction, everyone left in a heavy silence. The atmosphere was very somber. Some people wanted to speak to James, but they couldn't even decipher what to say.

Finally, James left with Lawrence and his father. They went back to his house so he could see Grace.

****

When they arrived, James faced Lawrence and Dani while his parents went to see Grace. James, needed to say some things to them he had not previously expressed.

"I owe you both such an apology. I'm sorry that you have to take over the church under such circumstances. I'm sorry that you have trusted me as your pastor and I have not done anything worthy of that trust."

James' throat was constricted, but he had to press forward.

"I'm sorry that I pursued Nylah in such a disrespectful manner and allowed myself to carry on with her for so long. I'm sorry we deceived you all this time. You are two of our closest friends. You didn't deserve this."

Dani got up and sat next to James. "James, we know you're sorry. We just want you to get back to the person God intended for you to be."

James glanced at her. "You're supposed to be angry with me."

"Maybe," Dani smiled. "You'll get plenty of that from others. You need our prayers, so that's what we're here for."

Lawrence sat on the other side of James and he and Dani wrapped their arms around him.

James tried to hold it, but he crumbled under their embrace.

"James, you have to fight through this," Lawrence whispered fiercely. "Don't give up."

"Why? Why have I done this? Why should God help me?" James cried.

"Because that's who He is. You need to learn how to lean on and trust in God. Now is the time for you to do that."

****

"Hi sweetheart," Katherine greeted, as she and Edward entered Grace's room.

"Hello," Grace returned. She was anxious to hear about the evening's events. "How did it go tonight?" she asked Edward.

Edward sighed thoughtfully. "He got through it, but it was rough. Nobody said anything tonight. But once it sinks in, we can expect for that to change."

"This is so ugly," Grace lamented. "I'm sorry we behaved so inexcusably bad."

"Grace honey, are you really sorry about your wrongdoing, or are you sorry that both of you got caught in this?"

Grace felt tears burning her eyes. "Both, at first. When I found out I was pregnant, I thought, man, if we could have just gotten married without incident, no one would have ever known James and I had been together for eight months. After that very thought, I knew this was why the situation had turned out the way it had. We were being exposed.

"I could handle the scorn better, when people didn't know James was the person I had been involved with. I am so internally embarrassed to go back to church now. I've been involved with my pastor for almost a year. How do I face them?"

"You have to lean totally on God. You can't run away from it. That is unfortunately the position the both of you have put yourselves in. Now it is time to deal with it," Edward said.

Grace nodded. "It means a lot to James that you both are here. To me, too."

"We love you both, honey," Katherine said.

Lawrence and Dani came in, saying that James wanted to speak with his parents. Edward and Katherine left and Lawrence and Dani sat in the empty seats.

"Grace, how do you feel?" Lawrence asked her.

"Anxious. How is James?"

"Not good," Dani said. "He is weighed down in a manner I never expected to see from him."

"He broke down while he was talking," Lawrence said. "I have never seen James break down like that before. The only other time he's come close was when you were in the hospital."

"These are his growing pains. It hurts him like crazy, but he'll be fine eventually, with the help of the Lord," Dani said.

Grace noticed Dani eyeing her. "What is it?" Grace asked her.

"Nothing. Just... Have you spoken to your family?" Dani inquired.

Grace took a deep, slow breath. "No. I don't need any stress."

"Gracie," Dani said, "They need to know what's going on with you."

Grace's eyes watered. "I know I should. I just can't right now. I'll get my mind together to talk to them before I have the baby. Just not right now. Can we change the subject, please?"

"Okay honey. Whatever you want," Dani said. Not wanting to upset Grace, they discussed a more pleasant subject until James was ready to see her.

****

"Mom, Dad; I need to apologize to you."

His parents sat close to him, which seemed to give him an air of moral support.

"I've made many poor decisions concerning my personal life and it's been going on for a long time. I apologize that I have not had much of a teachable spirit. I am sorry for this reproach—upon God and upon you."

Katherine took James' hand before she spoke. "James, we know that you are experiencing a lot of hurt and a lot of pain right now. We forgive you, but you're going to have to come to a place where you can forgive yourself."

"I feel broken," James told them, tears running down his face.

"Well, we know that the LORD is nigh unto them that are of a broken heart; and saveth such as be of a contrite spirit. I'd say you are well on your way, son," Edward said.

"James we are here for you and for Grace. God is always there for you. You need to decide what you want out of your life. You don't have to stay in this place that you're currently in. Surrender everything to Jesus. Lay it all on the altar, James. He knows what you need," Katherine encouraged.

****

James finally came to Grace's room, asking to speak with her alone. His face was arrested with heartache.

Grace whispered, instant tears forming, "Oh, James."

James couldn't even speak. He sat, placed his head in his hands and cried for several minutes. Grace couldn't move to comfort him; all she could do was cry with him until he was ready to talk. Her heart strings tugged for him. *He finally understands.*

James could barely catch his breath; his cries were deep. "Oh God, is this what you felt like?" James finally asked her. "This is awful. This is the worst I have ever felt in my entire life. I put you in a position to feel like this and made you go through it alone. I did that. How can you forgive me for that?"

"I can't—I can't hold that against you. It may have been poor judgment on your part, but I have also exercised poor judgment. We both made a choice. Now we have to deal with all the things that choice has brought upon us."

James' crying subsided, but he was silent for a long time. When he finally spoke, he asked Grace, "Do you think God will help us?"

"Do you honestly not know the answer to that?" Grace asked.

"I know He is sovereign. I just can't fathom that everything I have done can truly be forgiven."

"That's why He's the One who is faithful, merciful, kind and gracious. We have to remove ourselves so we can be found complete in Him."

"Are you trying to use my lines on me?" James asked. Grace saw the faintest hint of a smile.

"You know those aren't just lines. It's truth. We have to believe that God will help us. That's the only way we'll make it."

"We need to pray," James said. "Together."

Grace was surprised. Sad as it was to admit, this is the first time either one of them suggested that they join in prayer. Its place would have been foreign in the relationship they had before. Now it seemed principle.

Grace and James prayed together for a while before he left for the night. Right before she drifted off to sleep, all she remembered saying was, *"Please, God... please help us."*

Epilogue

Grace opened her eyes early Sunday morning. *Today is the day!* Grace was ecstatic. She and James were finally getting married, after morning service. Dani and Katherine would be with her and the men would come later.

Dani and Katherine made sure all the details for the ceremony were taken care of, asking Grace's input along the way. It was going to be a private ceremony, with few in attendance: Edward and Katherine; Lawrence and Dani; Lisa, her husband Spencer and Emma; Elder and Sister Rollins; and Kevin and Kara Fortson, the youth leaders at the church.

Earlier in the week, Dani had gone to a boutique that Grace frequently shopped at and explained about Grace not being able to leave the house, but she needed a dress to wear for the ceremony. They knew Grace personally, so they graciously extended a helping hand. They sent over two people with several dress choices in her size, so she could try them on and decide which she wanted. They also took various accessories: jewelry, bags, shoes and anything else that she might want to choose from.

They also offered to help in any way on the day before and of the ceremony, so Dani wouldn't have to do it all. With their help, in addition to Lisa and Katherine, Dani knew everything would be taken care of. The ceremony would take place in James' living room, which Dani could tell Grace must have decorated during the time she'd spent with James.

It was elegantly simple, with an understated class that was trademark Grace and Dani loved it. There weren't many other details regarding décor, but she still wanted the rest of the house to match the occasion.

They had a local favorite of James and Grace's come in to cater dinner and Lisa knew of a good bakery for the cake they would serve. Edward agreed to officiate, Spencer would play the piano James had in the living room and Kara and her brother were in charge of video/photography.

Grace heard a knock on the door. Dani popped her head in. "Good morning, Gracie! Are you up?"

"Come in!" Grace grinned.

"Are you excited?" Dani asked. Grace's face was lit up like a Christmas tree.

"Very. Is everything ready?"

"Yes, ma'am. Everybody has their various times for arrival. I'll be in and out to check on you and if you hear voices and whatnot, it's because I have people here to help set up. The girls from the boutique will help you get dressed. Your breakfast is almost ready so I want you to take it easy. You're excited, so even though it's a positive feeling, you still need to remain calm and not get overly worked up. Okay?"

"Thank you for taking care of me—and for all of your help with this."

"I must admit, once I got over my anger and really realized you were getting married, I became excited myself. I'm happy to do it for you."

Dani and Grace embraced before Dani reiterated her instructions for Grace to take it easy. Soon after, Grace's breakfast tray was brought in. There was a card on it and Grace thought it was from Dani, telling her again to be careful. Smiling as she opened it, tears sprang to her eyes as she read:

Nylah,

There are no words that can express my love for you. I have to be the most grateful man on earth to be blessed, in spite of myself, with such an amazing woman. You are everything I need, want and desire and that will remain forever. I can't wait to see you. I can't wait for you to finally be my wife. I anticipate our future. I thank God for you.

Love, James

Grace read and reread the card. *I have the opportunity to love him forever. I don't want to hurt him. God, we need your help for our marriage to work.* With that prayer, Grace was confident that they would receive God's help, if they continuously sought Him for it.

There was another knock on the door a little while later. Upon Grace's call to enter, Michelle stepped in.

"Michelle!" Grace gasped with delight. "James didn't tell me you were coming!"

Michelle smiled at Grace. They weren't by any means close, but she had always thought of her as a sweetheart since they first met years ago. "He didn't know," Michelle confirmed. "He'll be surprised to see us. I hope it's okay that we're here."

"Of course it is. James will be happy to see you. Thank you so much for coming."

"It's our pleasure. Rand came with me, but we didn't bring the girls. They can be pretty active, and I know you don't need that," Michelle chuckled. "But they're very excited to meet you, and pleased that they'll have a baby cousin soon. They said to tell Uncle James and Auntie Grace that they love you."

Grace was touched. It was going to be an emotional day. "They're so sweet. I can't wait to meet them. Please tell them Uncle James and Auntie Grace love them, too."

"I absolutely will. Now, I'm going to go help Dani and Mom, while you try and get some more rest. Please call us if you need anything at all." Michelle embraced a slightly tearful Grace before she left.

The next few hours seemed to pass quickly. Before she knew it, she was studying her reflection in a mirror, pushing back the threat of tears trying to force their way down.

"Gracie, you're beautiful," Dani whispered. Katherine didn't say anything because she was also trying not to cry. "Come on, it's time."

They escorted Grace outside to the hallway, where Elder Rollins was waiting. He was going to escort Grace down the aisle. Spencer was playing and Grace could see the others sitting as the ceremony started. Katherine went to her seat next to Michelle and then Dani entered.

When Grace appeared, James went from 0 to 1000, instantly. He had already been excited but seeing her intensified that feeling. To him, she was stunning. She always had a radiant glow to her, but there was a light in her eyes this time. She finally reached him and James took her hand, placing the other on her stomach. The baby kicked where his hand rested, provoking a chuckle out of him and smile out of Grace.

They expressed their vows to each other and finally, after months of pretending, they were officially pronounced husband and wife.

The rest of the afternoon was filled with cheerful conversation, great food and sounds of laughter that had not filled the house in a long time. James had been elated to see his sister and her husband. It meant a lot to him that she was able to come. With his family there, it felt like this was the beginning of true restoration for him and Grace. He knew the road ahead wouldn't be easy, but he was thankful for another chance.

Later on in the evening, after all of the guests had gone and cleanup was finished, Grace relaxed on the sofa, talking to Edward and Katherine. Dani, Lawrence, Rand and Michelle were with James making sure the house was set up the way he wanted. He wanted his first night home with Grace to be perfect. When they were finished, they joined his parents and Grace and they all sat around for a little while and talked. Dani and Lawrence finally decided to go home,

Michelle and Rand went to their hotel, and Edward and Katherine turned in for the night.

James turned to Grace. "I guess it's just us now."

Grace caressed his cheek. "I'm so glad you can stay with me now. I'm glad we can wake up next to each other and its okay. I'm glad you can kiss me at the park, or that we can hold hands at the store."

James smiled at her. "Is that all?" he teased.

"There's so much more," Grace affirmed, leaning in to kiss him.

He broke it before it went too far. He picked her up gently and said "time to go to our room." James carried her to the room, which was dimly lit with candles and soft music playing in the background.

"Oh James, I love it. But we can't—"

"I know. Don't worry, I didn't forget. It's just our first night together as husband and wife and I wanted it to be as special as possible." James set her down and eased her dress off of her. He removed all her undergarments and slipped her nightgown on her before placing her on the bed. After he changed, he set their refreshment cart close to the bed and settled in next to her.

Grace turned to him with an intense glow in her eyes.

"What is it?" James asked.

"Thank you for my card this morning. And by the way, I think you're going to be a wonderful husband."

"Your belief does a lot to calm my nerves about it. The last thing I want is another failed marriage."

"Well, I think I have a pretty good idea about who you are and what you're about. I don't intend to leave you anytime soon."

James kissed her with the knowledge that this time he was kissing his wife. She responded in kind until a smoldering heat was swirling around them. He lightly caressed her while trying to break their kiss. He finally pulled away from her. "Maybe we shouldn't get too carried away."

Grace snuggled up close to him and they talked about being married, the baby and their future until the candles burned out and they drifted off to sleep.
****

Here's a snippet from "The Next One": (this is not the real title)

Sunday morning after service, Lena bee-lined outside, headed to her car. She knew Harrison was somewhere around the church; she could sense his presence and she didn't feel like talking to him. She paused to note how she seemed to be changing. She didn't usually go out of her way to avoid anyone. She had never had a problem getting rid of anyone before. Then this man shows up and he seemed to be slowly infiltrating her life, much to her displeasure. She had, so far, been unsuccessful in getting him to back off.

She became aware of someone beside her and when she focused on the person, she inhaled deeply. "Harrison, what do you want?"

"I'm doing well, thank you. It's nice to see you, too. I'm escorting you to your car. Service was great wasn't it?" he smiled.

Lena would not be swayed or slowed down by his chatter. "You don't want to talk about service and I don't want to talk about service with you because you don't care. You've been pretending to be interested in the things around me for months. Quite frankly, I'm getting tired of it." Lena paused as they arrived at her car. Turning to face him she said, "Tell me what you want, or leave me alone."

Harrison smiled at her again and took a step closer to her. He leaned forward and whispered, inches from Lena's face, "I want your phone number and I want you to give it to me. If you don't, I'm going to kiss you in front of all these people."

Lena's eyes doubled in size as she realized how many people were outside the church building. She felt her car behind her and she really didn't have any escape. *I could scream, but that would cause undue embarrassment. I could kick him, but I don't know how he would respond. What am I going to do?*

Harrison knew he was taking a major risk in his outright threat to kiss her. Nothing else he had done these past few months had worked. He was actually feeling desperate to find a way past her walls. He could have left her alone, but what was the fun in that?

Lena knew he was serious enough to go through with his threat, and she would be embarrassed if he did. She would either give him her number just to get him away from her or she would take the kiss and possibly never talk to him again.

Harrison was willing to bet good money he would get her number for two reasons: she wouldn't want to suffer the embarrassment and she liked him.

She was externally resistant to his advances, but he felt she privately liked the attention he gave her. She was just having trouble admitting that to herself.

Lena conceded defeat this time and gave in. "Please, don't do that. I'll give you my number if it means that much to you." *If I give him what he wants now, what's to stop me from doing it again? This is trouble.* She mumbled her number just loud enough for him to hear.

Harrison was elated. It worked. "Thank you. I'll call you soon." He held her gaze long enough to make her blush. She shifted again as he grinned before turning and leaving.

About the Author

Erin Alexia originates from South Texas, but currently resides in the New England area. She has been writing for over 10 years, and has now decided to publish her first Christian Fiction series. Aside from writing, she is a part-time substitute teacher by day, and a full-time student by night. She's excited to be completing her undergraduate degree through Harvard University.

Her love for children inspires her to one day foster and/or adopt. Her love for travel enthuses her to see more of the world. Her love for God motivates her to live for Him daily. She sings for Jesus from her heart. And she is ever so grateful for the testimony God has given her.

Erin Alexia is working on her first seminar series entitled R.E.A.L. Writing. She's also active in ministry at her local church, serving in the choir, and contributing to youth ministry.

P.S. Check this out!

If you would like to enjoy delicious brownies like Grace and Dani, you can order them from The Brownie Shop at www.thebrownieshop.net. They are real and they are great!

Want to read Boaz is Dead? Head over to www.markmoorejr.com and order your digital copy today!

Thank you all so much for reading! I hope you enjoyed this story. Check back with us for the next installment of this Truth and Redemption series. Take care!

Made in the USA
Middletown, DE
25 February 2017